EA   HC

"Ready?" he asked under his breath.

When she nodded with reluctance she heard his sharp intake of breath.

"Maybe this will help."

He pulled her into his arms and found her mouth with a fierceness she wasn't prepared for, almost as if he was expecting her to fight him.

Stephanie clung to him, helpless to do anything else, and met the hunger of his kiss with an eagerness she would find embarrassing later. At last he was giving her a tender kiss, hot with desire, the one she'd been denied last night.

The way he was kissing her took her back to that unforgettable night on Grand Turk, when they'd given each other everything with a matchless joy she couldn't put into words. He pressed her against the doorjamb to get closer. One kiss after the other made her crazy with desire. Stephanie was so in love with Nikos nothing existed for her but to love him and be loved.

Dear Reader

When most readers hear the words Navy SEAL they think of the American military. But the Greek military also has its Navy SEALs. In fact they have a reputation for being some of the fiercest and most well-trained men in the world. If you want to see them in action, go to the website below to watch a short video: http://www.youtube.com/watch?v=inSFmHhEs10

In THE GREEK'S TINY MIRACLE gorgeous Nikos Vassalos has put in his time with the Navy SEALs, but when Floridian Stephanie Marsh meets him for the first time she thinks he's an exporter from New York. As their story unfolds, and she seeks him out several months later, the layers of both their lives will be peeled back to expose secrets that will send chills and thrills through you.

Enjoy!

Rebecca Winters

THE GREEK'S
TINY MIRACLE

BY
REBECCA WINTERS

Published in Great Britain 2014
by Mills & Boon, an imprint of Harlequin (UK) Limited,
Eton House, 18-24 Paradise Road, Richmond, Surrey, TW9 1SR

© 2014 Rebecca Winters

ISBN: 978 0 263 24152 5

Harlequin (UK) Limited's policy is to use papers that are natural,
renewable and recyclable products and made from wood grown in
sustainable forests. The logging and manufacturing processes conform
to the legal environmental regulations of the country of origin.

Printed and bound in Great Britain
by CPI Antony Rowe, Chippenham, Wiltshire

Rebecca Winters, whose family of four children has now swelled to include five beautiful grandchildren, lives in Salt Lake City, Utah, in the land of the Rocky Mountains. With canyons and high alpine meadows full of wildflowers, she never runs out of places to explore. They, plus her favourite vacation spots in Europe, often end up as backgrounds for her romance novels, because writing is her passion, along with her family and church.

Rebecca loves to hear from readers. If you wish to e-mail her, please visit her website: www.cleanromances.com

Recent books by Rebecca Winters:

MARRY ME UNDER THE MISTLETOE**
A MARRIAGE MADE IN ITALY
ALONG CAME TWINS…*
BABY OUT OF THE BLUE*
THE COUNT'S CHRISTMAS BABY
THE RANCHER'S HOUSEKEEPER
A BRIDE FOR THE ISLAND PRINCE
SNOWBOUND WITH HER HERO

*Tiny Miracles
**Gingerbread Girls

These books are also available in eBook format from www.millsandboon.co.uk

To my talented daughter Dominique,
a writer for Harlequin herself, who has put up with
her *outre* writer mom and encouraged her
through thick and thin. How lucky can I be?

CHAPTER ONE

April 27

EVERY TIME MORE hotel guests entered the beachfront resort restaurant on Grace Bay in the Turks and Caicos Islands in the Caribbean, Stephanie expected to see her black-haired Adonis appear. That was how she thought of Dev Harris.

After their fantastic ninety-foot dive to Elephant Ear Canyon that afternoon to see the huge sponges, the tall, powerfully built New Yorker, who resembled a Greek god, had whispered that he'd meet her in the dining room at eight for dinner. They'd watch the sunset *and later, each other.*

As he'd helped her out of the dive boat, giving her arm a warm squeeze, his eyes, black as jet, conveyed the words he didn't speak in front of the others in their scuba diving group. He was living for another night with her like last night.

She'd reluctantly left him to go to the beachfront condo and get ready for dinner. Her silvery-gold hair needed a shampoo. She'd decided to wear it loose from a side part. Time with the blow dryer and a brush brought out the natural curl, causing it to flow across her shoulders.

With the golden tan she'd picked up, tonight she'd chosen to wear a blue sleeveless sundress. She wanted to look beautiful for him. Last night she'd worn a filmy tangerine-colored dress and had bought a shimmering lip gloss to match. He'd told her that, in the dying rays of the sun, she'd look like a piece of golden fruit he longed to devour very slowly and thoroughly.

Her body trembled just remembering those words. While she waited for him to come, the memory of the way he'd made love to her over and over again made it difficult to breathe. It was her first intimate experience with a man, and had happened so naturally she felt as if she was living in a dream, one from which she never wanted to awaken.

In ten days' time Stephanie had fallen so deeply in love, her whole world had changed. Throughout her dating years she'd had various boyfriends. Just last week she'd gone on a date with a guy named Rob Ferris, who ran an auto parts franchise, but she knew when he took her home after dinner that she really wasn't interested in a second date.

Then she met Dev. The first time she'd seen him walking toward the boat with the dive master, her breath had caught. When their gazes collided, that was it. The feeling she'd been waiting for all her adult life.

Other relationships with past boyfriends had nothing to do with the profound kind of love she felt for the sophisticated thirty-two year-old bachelor, who'd told her he was in the international exporting business. He blew away every other man in existence.

Her three girlfriends who'd arranged their April

vacations to come on this scuba diving trip with her fully agreed he was out-of-this-world gorgeous. Melinda thought he must be one of those frogmen from the military, the way he maneuvered under the water. He was certainly built like one.

Stephanie agreed with her friends, but there was more to Dev than his physical attributes and diving skills. Much more. Everything he said and did revealed that he was well-traveled and educated, making him exceptional, and so charismatic she could hardly breathe when she thought about him.

Where was he? By now it was quarter to nine. Obviously, he'd been held up. The only thing to do was go back to her room and call him on the hotel land line. His beachfront condo, where they'd spent last night, was located on the other side of the restaurant, but she thought she should phone him first.

Stephanie was on her way out when a waiter came toward her with a florist box in his hands. "Ms. Walsh? This is for you, with Mr. Harris's compliments."

Thrilled to have received it, she went back to the table to take off the lid. He was probably on his way to her now. Inside the tissue was a corsage of gardenias with a card.

Thank you for the most memorable ten days and nights of my life, Stephanie. Your sweetness is like these gardenias and I'll never forget you. Unfortunately, I've had to leave the island because of an emergency at my work that couldn't be handled by anyone else. Enjoy the rest of your trip and be safe flying back to Crystal River. I miss you already. Dev.

Stephanie sat there and felt the blood drain from her face.

Her spring idyll was over.

He'd already driven to the airport to catch his flight to New York. *Of course* he hadn't left her a phone number or address, nor had he asked her for the same information. On purpose he hadn't given her a shred of hope that they'd ever see each other again.

She had to be the biggest fool who'd ever lived.

No, there was one other person she knew who shared that honor. Her mother, who'd died from cancer after Stephanie had graduated from college. Twenty-four years ago Ruth Walsh had made the same mistake with an irresistible man. But whoever he was hadn't stuck around once the fun was over, either. Stephanie didn't know his name and had no memories of him, only that her mother had said he was good-looking, exciting and an excellent skier.

He and Dev were two of a kind.

Stephanie closed her eyes tightly. How many females went off on vacation and supposedly met their soul mate, who swept them off their feet, only to abandon them once the excitement wore off? It had to be in the hundreds of thousands, if not the millions. Stephanie, like her mother, was one of those pathetic statistics who'd gotten caught up in the rapture.

White-hot with anger for being in her mid-twenties before learning the lesson she should have had memorized early in life, because of her birth father, Stephanie shot out of the chair. As she passed the waiter, she gave him a couple dollars and told him to get rid of the things she'd left on the table.

Stephanie didn't know about her friends, but she

couldn't possibly stay on the island for the last four days of their trip. Tomorrow morning she'd be on the first plane back to Florida. If a man was too good to be true, then shame on the woman who believed she was the first female to beat the odds.

Dev was so attractive there had to be trails of broken-hearted females around the scuba diving world who knew exactly what it was like to lie in his arms and experience paradise, only to wake up and discover he'd moved on.

He'd told her that scuba diving was his favorite form of recreation. What he hadn't mentioned was that womanizing went hand in hand with his favorite pastime. It was humiliating to think she was one of those imbeciles who didn't have the sense to take one look at him and run far away as fast as possible.

Too furious for tears, she returned to the condo, thankful her roommates were still out. They'd probably gone into town to party with some of the other tourists staying at the resort. That gave Stephanie time to change her flight reservation and pack without them asking a lot of questions.

By tomorrow afternoon she'd be back on the job. Stephanie loved her work. Right now she was planning on it saving her life.

If she let herself think about those long walks with Dev, past the palms and Casuarina trees while they were entwined in each other's arms, she'd go mad.

July 13

"Captain Vassalos?"

Nikos had just finished putting on the jacket of his

uniform—the last time he would wear it. Steadying himself with his crutches, he looked around in time to see Vice Admiral Eugenio Prokopios of the Aegean Sea Naval Command in Piraeus, Greece, enter his hospital room and shut the door. The seasoned Greek naval hero was an old friend of his father and grandfather.

"This is an honor, sir."

"Your parents are outside waiting for you. I told them I wanted to come in first to see you. After your last mission, we can be thankful the injury to your spine didn't paralyze you, after all."

Thankful?

Nikos cringed. His last covert operation with Special Forces had wiped out the target, but his best friend, Kon, had been killed. As for Nikos, his doctor told him he would never be the man he once was. His spine ought to heal in time, but he'd never be 100 percent again, and couldn't stay in the Greek military as a SEAL, not when he would probably suffer episodes of PTSD for a long time, maybe even years.

He'd been getting counseling and was taking a serotonin reuptake inhibitor to help him feel less worried and sad, but he'd had several nightmares. They left him feeling out of control and depressed.

"Now that you're being released from the hospital this morning, it won't be long before you won't need those crutches."

Nikos hated the sight of them. "I'm planning on getting rid of them as soon as possible."

"But not until you've had a good long rest after your ordeal."

"A good long rest" was code for one reality. The part

of his life that had brought challenge and purpose was finished. Only blackness remained.

"I don't expect it to take that much time, sir."

After a two and a half months' hospitalization, Nikos knew exactly why the vice admiral had shown up. This was his father's work. He'd been thwarted when Nikos had joined the military, and expected his son to return to the family business. Now that he was incapacitated, his father had sent his good friend Eugenio to wish him well with a pep talk about getting back in the family fold.

The older man eyed him solemnly. "Our navy is grateful for the heroic service you've rendered in Special Forces. You're a credit to your family and our country. Your father is anxious for you to resume your place with your brother at the head of Vassalos Shipping so he can retire."

His father would never retire.

Vice Admiral Prokopios had just let Nikos know—in the kindest way, of course—that though his military service was over, the family business was waiting to embrace him again. Of course, the older man knew nothing about Nikos's history with his father, or he would never have said what he did.

Until after Nikos was born and turned out to be a Vassalos, after all, his father hadn't believed he was his son, all because of a rumor that turned out to have no substance. The experience had turned him into a bitter, intransigent man. The damage inflicted on the Vassalos marriage carried over to the children, and had blighted Nikos's life.

The navy turned out to be his escape from an impossible situation. But ten years later it was back in triplicate.

He was thirty-two years of age, and everything was over.

Sorrow weighed him down at the loss of Kon Gregerov. Nikos's best friend from childhood, who'd come from a wonderful family on nearby Oinoussa Island, had joined the navy with him. The man had been like a brother, and had helped keep Nikos sane and grounded during those tumultuous years while he fought against his father's domination, among other things.

He and Kon had plans to go into their own business together once they'd retired from the military, but his friend had been blown up in the explosion that almost killed Nikos.

It should have been me.

"I'm sorry you were forced to leave Providenciales unexpectedly to perform your last covert operation. So when you're ready, we'll send you back there for more rest and relaxation."

Nikos's stomach muscles clenched at the mere mention of Providenciales. That experience had been like a fantastic dream, one he'd relived over and over on those nights in the hospital when he wasn't suffering flashbacks. To go back there again without *her* would kill him. After what had happened to him, there could be no Stephanie Walsh in his life. He was going in another direction entirely.

"Nikos?" the vice admiral prodded.

"Thank you for the kind offer, but I'd rather recuperate at home."

"If that's your wish."

"It is."

"Then I'll say goodbye for now. Be assured I'm mighty proud of you. Good luck."

They saluted before he left the room. Moments later one of the hospital staff entered with a wheelchair. As Nikos sat down, his parents swept into the room. They'd been constant visitors, but they hovered until he felt he would choke.

"Darling!" his mother exclaimed, and hugged him before carrying his crutches for him. "You look wonderful despite your weight loss. Once we get you home, we'll fatten you up in no time. Your grandparents are elated and your sister and Timon have already arrived with the children to welcome you back."

"This is a great day, son." His exultant father embraced him before reaching for his luggage. "Leon's eager to talk business with you."

Nikos had no intention of working in the family business like his elder brother, and his father knew it. But his dad never let up about anything, and it had driven a wedge between them that couldn't be breached. However, now wasn't the time to get into it. The three of them moved out of the room and down the corridor.

"How did it go with Eugenio?"

As if his father didn't know. "Fine."

They emerged from the main doors of the hospital under a blue sky. Once they were settled inside the limousine, his father said, "We've been waiting for this day. So has Natasa. She and her parents will be joining us tomorrow evening for a small party."

Nikos's anger flared. "Then *uninvite* them. You might as well know that after tonight, I'll be living on the *Diomedes* while I get my strength back." He was sick of visitors and hospital staff. He needed to be completely alone and didn't want anyone to know his activities. His boat would be his refuge from now on.

"You can't do that to us *or* to her!" his father thundered. "You've put this situation with Natasa on hold for long enough. A marriage between the two of you has been understood for years. She's expecting it now that you're home for good. Your mother and I want you to give us grandchildren. We've waited long enough."

Their families had been best friends for years. His sister, Gia, and Natasa Lander had always been close. It had been an impossible situation he'd been happy to get out of when he'd joined the military.

"Then that's a pity, because I never made love to her or asked her to marry me. She should have moved on years ago." She was attractive enough and would have made a good wife and mother, but he'd never been on fire for her. Thank heaven he hadn't made the mistake of sleeping with her. After meeting Stephanie, the thought of Natasa or any another woman was anathema to him. "Now that I'm out of the hospital, I need to go my own way."

"But that's absurd! She's in love with you."

"It's a moot point, since I'm not in love with her and never have been. Any hope you had for me marrying her is out of the question. I'm deadly serious about this."

His father's cheeks grew ruddy with emotion. "You don't know what you're saying!"

"But I do. Natasa is a lovely person, but not the one for me." Unless she had an agenda of her own, there was something wrong with her for waiting around for him this long. "At this point I'm afraid a marriage between the two of us is only a figment of your and her parents' imagination."

"How dare you say that!" his father muttered furiously.

"How dare *you?*" Nikos retorted back. "You'll be doing her a favor if you tell her and her family that I'm not well enough to see anyone now. Hopefully, they'll finally get the point! Don't turn this into a nightmare for me or you'll wish you hadn't!"

Nikos had suffered too many of them since the fishing vessel with all the surveillance equipment, along with Kon, had been blown out of the water by the enemy. If Nikos hadn't happened to be over the side, checking the hull for damage because of a run earlier in the day, he wouldn't still be alive.

As it was, he'd been found unconscious in the water. The doctors at the hospital hadn't given him a chance of walking again due to the damage to his lower spine, but they'd been proved wrong. He'd come out of it with deep bruising and reduced mobility. No one could say how much he would heal with time.

"We can discuss this later," his mother said, always anxious to mollify his father. For as long as Nikos could remember, she'd tried to keep peace between them. Though he loved her for it, the ugly history with his father had dictated that certain things would never change....

"There's nothing to discuss."

His military career was over. Life as he'd known it was over. Nikos was living for the moment when he could be away from everyone. Both his parents crowded him until he felt stifled, but he knew he had to endure this until tomorrow morning.

He'd already made arrangements with Yannis, who would come to the house and drive him to the marina in Nikos's car. Once on board the *Diomedes,* he intended to stay put. Drinking himself to death sounded better and better.

Silence invaded the vehicle until they reached the small airport in Athens. Nikos took a fortifying breath as he stepped out and reached for his crutches to board his father's private jet. The steward knew him well and nodded to him. "Welcome home, Nikos."

"Thank you, Jeno."

"Are you hungry?"

"No."

"Some tea?"

"How about a beer?"

The other man smiled. "Coming right up."

Nikos found a seat in the club compartment with his parents, who for once had gone quiet. He put the crutches on the floor and fastened himself in. It was a short forty-minute flight across the Aegean to Chios. From there they'd take the helicopter to Vassalos Shipping on Egnoussa, where they'd land and drive home.

He stared blindly out the window until fatigue took over, causing him to lounge back in the seat and close his eyes. The mention of marriage had triggered thoughts of a certain female in another part of the world he'd had to leave two and half months ago—so abruptly he still hadn't recovered from the pain.

Stephanie Walsh would have received the gardenias with his note. It would have sent a dagger straight to her heart. Nikos knew how it felt, because when he'd had his farewell gift delivered to the restaurant, he'd experienced gut-wrenching pain over what he'd been forced to do.

His hand formed a fist, because there hadn't been a damn thing he'd been able to do to comfort her at the time. As a navy SEAL, everything about his life was classified. Since then his whole world had been turned upside down, ensuring he would never seek her out again.

From the second he'd first met the beautiful American woman on the beach, her appeal had been so strong he couldn't find the strength to stay away from her. Knowing his leave was for only two weeks, he hadn't intended to get involved with her. Because he'd be returning shortly to join his unit, there could be no future in it.

Every day he kept telling himself he'd go to another resort on the island to keep his distance, but every day he grew more enamored of her. The night with her before he'd received orders to return to Greece should never have happened.

He loathed himself for allowing things to get that far, but she'd been like a fever in his blood. Intoxicated by her beauty, by everything about her, he'd given in to his desires, and she'd been right there with him. Her loving response had overwhelmed him, setting him on fire.

There'd been other women in his life, but never again would he know a night of passion like that. What he and Stephanie had shared for those ten precious days had been unbelievable. His longing for her was still so real he could taste it.

When he'd awakened on their last morning together, they'd been tangled up in each other's arms. She'd looked at him with those sapphire eyes, willing him to love her, and he'd wanted to stay in that bed with her forever. After their dive that afternoon, it had shredded him to walk away from her and board the jet for the flight to Athens, but he'd had his orders. He couldn't imagine a world that didn't include her.

After meeting up with Kon for their next covert operation, Nikos had confided his deepest feelings, telling him that after this last mission was completed, he planned to resign his commission and marry her. But just three days after that, the enemy had struck, and his best friend was dead. Nikos was no longer a whole man. Stephanie could be only a memory to him now.

En route to the Caribbean he'd never dreamed he would meet the woman who would leave her mark on him. His mind went over the conversation he'd just had with his father.

You don't know what you're saying!

But I do. Natasa is a lovely person, but there's something wrong with a woman who waits around for a man who's never been interested in her romantically. I'm afraid a marriage between the two of us is out of the question.

Nikos had met the ideal woman meant for him, but she would have to remain in his dreams. If Kon were still alive he'd say, "Get in touch with her and tell her the truth about your condition. You trusted her enough to spend every living moment with her. It might ease the pain for both of you if she knew who you really were, and what happened to you."

A groan escaped Nikos's throat. With his spinal injury, he wasn't the same man she'd met. Part of the collateral damage had rendered him sterile. He'd never be able to give a woman a child from his own body. Nikos lived in a dark world now. He looked and felt like hell. No woman would want a man whose flashbacks could make him dangerous to himself and others. Stephanie would only hate him for lying to her. For using her for pleasure, then dumping her without explanation.

"Nikos?"

His eyes flew open. "Jeno?"

The steward looked at him with compassion. "Are you feeling ill? Can I get you anything?"

He shook his head. He'd come to a dead end. The woman he loved and desired was permanently beyond his reach now.

"We're getting ready to descend."

"Thank you."

He fastened his seat belt. Jeno was right about one thing: Nikos did feel ill. The meeting with the vice admiral was like the first handful of dirt thrown on top of the coffin. He saw the life he'd once known vanish into the void, leaving him to travel through a tunnel of blackness that had no end....

July 26

Stephanie was going to be a mother.

She ran a hand over her stomach, which had grown fuller, making it harder to fasten the top two buttons of her jeans. It still seemed unbelievable that she was carrying Dev's child. When she'd missed her period last month it hadn't alarmed her, because she'd always been irregular. In college she'd gone six months without a period.

But over the last three weeks she'd felt weak and

nauseated. In her depressed state she'd lost her appetite and thought she had a flu bug. But it didn't go away and then she started noticing other changes to her body. It all added up to one thing, and the home pregnancy test yesterday had turned out positive, shocking the daylights out of her.

The trip to Dr. Sanders today had confirmed that she was three months along with Dev's baby. *Incredible.* Her OB had ordered pills for her nausea, plus iron and prenatal vitamins to build her up.

If she caught up to Dev, would he want to know he was going to be a father?

Deep down, she'd been waiting for him to contact her. He knew she worked for Crystal River Water Tours. It would have been easy enough for him to call and leave a message. But that hadn't happened. He hadn't planned on ever seeing or talking to her again.

Yet she felt certain the man she'd fallen in love with would have wanted to hear the truth about his own baby. But it seemed that man didn't exist. If she were able to find him, would he still tell her he wanted nothing to do with her or the baby, once he found out?

For the next twelve hours she agonized about what to do, vacillating over the decision she needed to make. By morning, one thing overshadowed every consideration. She knew her child would want to know its father. It would be the most important thing in her baby's life.

Stephanie knew all about that, having always longed to meet her birth father and know his name. It took two to make a child, and it was up to her to inform Dev if it was at all possible. What he did with the information was up to him.

But her hand hesitated before she reached for the phone to begin her inquiries at the resort. The two people she knew there might wonder why she needed information. They'd probably deduce she was some obsessed girlfriend.

How humiliating would it be to confide the truth about the baby to them? She just couldn't. But maybe it would work if she explained she'd been worrying about him ever since he'd disappeared, the very night they were going to have dinner together. She felt certain he'd been ill, thus the reason for his swift departure. Did they know any way she might get in touch with him, just to see if he was all right?

With her hand shaking, she called the number on the brochure she'd kept, and waited.

"Dive shop. This is Angelo."

She gripped the cell phone tighter. "Hello, Angelo. I'm glad it's you. I tried to reach you earlier, but you were out. This is Stephanie Walsh. You probably don't remember me. I was there almost three months ago."

"Stephanie? I always remember the pretty girls, you especially."

Her heart beat too fast. "You just made my day."

He laughed. "You had a good time on vacation?"

"Wonderful, thanks to you." *The best of my whole life until the box of gardenias was brought to the table.*

"That's good. How can I help you?"

"I'm trying to reach Dev Harris, the scuba diver from New York I partnered with that first week. Do you have a phone number or an email for him? Anything at all to help me? He left so suddenly, I've worried over the last few months that he might have been taken ill. I have pictures I'd like to send him via email."

"Let me check. Don't hang up."

"No. I won't."

She paced the bedroom of her condo while she waited. There were a lot of Devlin, Devlon or Devlan Harrises listed in New York City, but none she could reach was the man she was trying to find.

When she'd first gotten back to Florida, anger had driven her to phone New York information, but there was no such name listed for him. She'd spent several days phoning exporting companies where he might be working, but she'd turned up nothing.

After exhausting that avenue, she'd called various airlines that had landed planes on the island April 18, but got no help. The resort could tell her only what she already knew, that he was from New York. That was when she'd given up. But her pregnancy had changed everything.

"Stephanie? I'm back. Sorry, but there is no address or phone number. Perhaps one of the shops you visited would know something."

She bit her lip in disappointment. "We didn't do any shopping, but he did have some flowers delivered to me. Would they have come from the resort?"

"No, no. The Plant Shop in town. Just a minute and I'll give you the number." She held her breath while she waited. "Yes. Here it is."

Stephanie wrote it down. "You live up to your name, Angelo. Thank you so much."

"You're welcome. Good luck finding him."

After hanging up, she placed the call. Stephanie had once told him she loved gardenias. Tears stung her eyes. She had to admit his parting gift had been done with a certain style, while at the same time destroying her dreams. If there were no results, then the baby she was carrying would never know its father.

"The Plant Shop."

"Hello. My name is Stephanie Walsh. I'm calling from Florida. On April 27 a box of gardenias from your shop was delivered to me at the Palm Resort. I never did get to thank the gentleman who sent it to me. He left before I realized he'd gone. His name was Dev Harris. Could you give me an address or a phone number, please? He's from New York City. That's all I know."

It was a long shot, but she was desperate.

"I'm sorry, but we can't give out that information."

"Can you at least tell me what time he left the order?"

"Just a moment and I'll check." After a minute, the salesclerk returned. "It was phoned in at 5:00 p.m."

"Thank you for your help."

After she hung up, one more idea flitted through her mind. She called the resort again and asked if she could speak to Delia, the darling girl who'd been the maid for their rooms. Could Delia call Stephanie back collect, please? It was very important.

The front desk said they'd give her the message. Within a half hour, Stephanie's phone rang and it was the resort calling. Delia was on the other end.

"Hello, Stephanie."

"Oh, Delia. Thanks so much for calling me back."

"Of course. How is the handsome Dev?"

I wish I knew. "Actually, I'm not sure. I'm really worried about him. That's why I've phoned you. I'm thinking he must have left the island early because he was ill and didn't want me to know or worry. I thought

I would have heard from him by now, and need your help to find him if it's at all possible."

"Tell you what. My boyfriend works at the airport servicing the planes before takeoff. I'll ask him to find out what planes took off on April 27 after five in the evening. Perhaps he'll learn something that can help you."

"I'll make this worth your while, Delia."

"I would like to do this for you. I never saw two people more in love."

Tears scalded Stephanie's eyes. "Thank you," she whispered. "I just hope he isn't fatally ill."

"I don't blame you for being upset."

Whether Delia believed her excuse for calling or not, Stephanie couldn't worry about that now.

Two hours later her phone rang again. "Stephanie? He couldn't get you names, but there were three flights out that evening, if this helps. One was a nonstop flight to Los Angeles, California, another nonstop to Vancouver, British Columbia. The last was a private jet owned by the Vassalos Corporation, headed for Athens, Greece."

She blinked.

None of the planes had headed due north to New York. Her spirits plunged. If he'd been called back to his work on an emergency, surely he would have taken a direct flight to New York. There were dozens of them leaving the Caribbean for that destination.

"You're an angel for being willing to help me, Delia. Expect a thank-you in the mail for you and your boyfriend from me."

Stephanie rang off, shaking with the knowledge that Dev had lied to her without compunction. *Who are you, mystery man?* Had he pulled a fictitious name out of a hat on the spur of the moment? Was Dev a nickname?

One thing she was convinced of at this point: he was no New Yorker. And he'd been in an enormous hurry when he'd left Providenciales. Thousands of business-men traveled by private jet. Certainly if he'd needed to leave before they'd even had dinner, it would make sense he had his own special mode of transportation waiting. No long lines...

Before she did anything else, she went to her com-puter in the den of the condo she'd inherited from her mother, to make a global search of the name Vassalos in Greece. One source came up more prominent than all the rest and drew her attention. *Vassalos Maritime Shipping, Egnoussa, Greece.*

Shipping...

After more searches she discovered the Oinousses, a group of small islands in the eastern Aegean Sea near Turkey. Egnoussa, the largest inhabited one, was fourteen kilometers long. One of Greece's most im-portant naval academies was based there, due to the rich seafaring history of the islands. A smaller island, Oinoussa, was also inhabited.

Reading further, she learned Egnoussa was home to some of the richest shipping magnate families in the world. There were only four hundred or so inhab-itants, with some fabulous mansions. A naval com-mercial academy and museum were located on one part of the island.

She replayed the memories of Dev in her mind. His urbane sophistication and knowledge set him apart from other men she'd known. He'd possessed a natu-ral authority and spoke impeccable English. But when she thought about it, she realized he hadn't sounded like a New Yorker.

Had he come from a Greek island? If so, he would naturally be at home in the water.

He'd told her he worked for an international exporting company in New York. Did that company have an outlet in Greece? Did Dev work for it? Exporting could translate to mean shipping, couldn't it? In her mind it wasn't a far stretch to see where he might have come up with his lie.

What if Egnoussa was his home? Was he from *that* Vassalos family, with the kind of wealth that had opened every door for him? Maybe this was a stab in the dark, but the more she thought about him, the more the shoe seemed to fit. The cliché about looking like a Greek god fit him like a second skin.

She could phone the shipping company and ask questions. But since he obviously didn't want to be found, if he was there or got wind that she was trying to reach him, she might never get answers. Scrolling down farther, she found more information.

After a short flight from Athens to the island of Chios, an hour's boat ride takes you to Egnoussa Island. There's one hotel with only twelve rooms, one taxi. You can walk Egnoussa in a day.

Her mind reeled with ideas. She could take some pictures of him with her and show them to someone at the shipping office. Stephanie would know immediately if that person recognized him. Maybe she was a fool, but for her baby's sake she had to try to find him, and would use some of her savings to get there.

Stephanie called the doctor to make certain it was okay to fly. He told her she'd be all right for twenty-eight weeks. After that, she'd need to check with him about it. Since Greece didn't require immunizations for visitors from the United States, she'd be all right.

Luckily, she already had a passport. When she and her friends had decided to vacation together, they'd applied for passports in case they decided on a vacation along the French or Italian Riviera. But in the end, the Caribbean had won out.

If she traveled to Greece and it turned out to be a fruitless mission, then so be it. Whatever happened, the sooner she went, the better for her state of mind. Unlike her mother, who didn't attempt to tell her lover he was a father, at least Stephanie could explain to her child that she'd done everything humanly possible to locate the man who'd called himself Dev Harris.

Life was going to be difficult enough from here on out. She would have to discuss her condition with her boss. If he could give her a front desk job until after the baby was born, she'd be thankful and grateful. But if not, she'd need to start looking for another kind of job after she got back from Greece. Besides finishing paying off the mortgage, she needed to earn enough money to provide for herself and the baby.

CHAPTER TWO

July 28

NIKOS HAD BEEN out on the *Diomedes* for two weeks, but this afternoon he'd docked at the marina in Egnoussa. As soon as he replenished his food supply, he'd be leaving again. To his chagrin, he still needed support to move around, but had traded in his crutches for a cane. He used it only when he was exceptionally tired.

His right-hand man, Yannis, a seaman who'd worked for the family for over forty years, had just finished tying the ropes when Nikos's silver-haired father approached them.

"Where have you been, Nikos?"

"Where I've been every day and night since I was released from the hospital, exercising and swimming off shore." Battling his PTSD.

Despite taking medication, he'd had two violent episodes flashing back to the explosion. According to his doctor, with the passage of time they'd start to slow down, but it might take months or even years. For the time being Nikos had made the small custom-built yacht his home, where no one except Yannis could be witness.

What his family didn't know was that some of his time had been spent with Kon's grieving parents. He'd also had long talks with Kon's married brother, Tassos, about many things. He was only a year older than Nikos and lived on Oinoussa, an island close to Egnoussa. Before Kon's death the three of them had been close.

Tassos had gone into oil engineering and had recently returned after working on an oil rig in the southern Aegean. He had a brilliant head on his shoulders. He and Nikos had been talking a lot about Greece's financial crisis and the direction of the country. For the time being Nikos mostly listened to Tassos, but he could scarcely concentrate while he felt half-alive.

"I've been phoning you for the last hour! Why didn't you answer?" His father had to be upset to have come down to the dock.

"I was doing some shopping with Yannis, who's bringing things on board from the car. What's wrong?" His father looked flustered.

"You have a visitor."

"If you mean Natasa, you're wasting your time."

"No. Someone else."

"I can't imagine who could be so important it would send you here." Since returning home from the hospital, Nikos had stayed in touch with his family by phone, but he'd seen no one except Kon's family and Yannis.

His father's eyes, dark like his own, studied him speculatively. "Does this woman look familiar to you?"

He reached in his pocket and pulled out two snapshots. One showed Nikos and Stephanie in the dive boat. They'd just removed their gear and were smiling at each other. His breath caught at how beautiful she was. Angelo had taken the picture.

The other photo showed them on the beach with their arms around each other, right after the sun had set. In that sundress she'd looked like a piece of golden fruit. In fact that's what he'd told her, among other things. The girl Delia, in housekeeping, had taken their picture.

"I take it she's the woman who has erased thoughts of Natasa from your mind."

Nikos could hear his father talking, but at the sight of Stephanie in those photos, he reeled so violently he almost fell off the pier into the water. She was here on the island? But that was impossible! There was no way on earth she could have found him.

"You were careless to allow yourself to be photographed in the Caribbean while you were still in active service. What is she to you, Nikos? Answer me."

He couldn't. He was still trying to grasp the fact that she'd flown to Greece and known exactly where to come.

"After looking at these pictures," his father continued, "I've decided you're in much deeper than I thought. Her beauty goes without saying, and she has a breathless innocence that could fool any man. Even *you,* my son."

Nikos closed his eyes tightly.

"You've never looked at Natasa or any woman the way you're looking at this female viper. I admit she's devilishly ravishing in that American way, but she's a mercenary viper nonetheless, one who knows your monetary worth and has come to trap you.

"Surely after what happened to Kon years ago, you realize that getting involved with a foreign woman on vacation in those surroundings can only mean one thing. Don't let her get you any more ensnared. I know you well enough that if she's pregnant, it's someone else's."

His father's words twisted the knife deeper. The mention of Kon's tragedy brought back remembered pain. Was history repeating itself with Nikos? This just wasn't possible! No one in the Caribbean knew Nikos or anything about him. *No one.*

He rubbed the back of his neck. "Do you mean she simply walked into the building?"

"Like she knew the place, according to Ari," his father explained. "After arriving in the taxi, she approached him at the front desk and asked to speak to Mr. Vassalos. When she showed Ari the pictures, he phoned me at home. I told him to have her taken into my office, where she's waiting for word of you."

Nikos still couldn't believe it. For a number of reasons this seemed completely out of character for Stephanie. He could have sworn she was the one woman in his life who gave everything without wanting anything back. While he'd been diving with her, he'd trusted her with his life, and she him. Or so he'd thought. To have been so wrong about her gutted him in an agonizing way.

"Have you made a commitment to her?"

They'd made love all night, transforming his world.

"Though it's none of your business, the answer is no," he muttered in a gravelly voice, poleaxed by this revelation. Not then, and since the explosion that had blown his dreams to hell, *most definitely not now...*

After receiving the gardenias, the Stephanie he thought he'd known would never have come searching for him. She would have understood the gesture meant goodbye, but apparently that hadn't deterred her from what she wanted.

How had she found him? Was it his money she was after? He'd taken precautions, ruling out pregnancy as a factor. But as his father had said, she could be pregnant by someone else. The very accusation he'd turned on Nikos's mother, ruining their lives. The notion that Stephanie had been after Nikos for his money made him feel ill.

"It's little wonder you've displayed such indifference to Natasa. What do you intend to do?"

Just when Nikos thought life couldn't get worse, *it had.*

He stared at his father. "Nothing." He handed him back the photos. "Give Ari instructions to tell her I'm out of the country and won't be back."

"No personal message?"

"None." He bit out the word.

A gleam of satisfaction entered his father's eyes. His parent still had this sick fantasy about Nikos and Natasa. "I'll take care of it."

Stephanie sat in the chair, actually stunned that her intuition had paid off. The second she'd shown the photographs to the man in reception, she'd seen the way his eyes had flared in surprise.

The next thing she knew, he'd made a phone call and said something in Greek she couldn't understand. Before long he'd escorted her to an office down the hall filled with pictures of ships of all kinds, almost like a museum of navigational history. The man told her they were trying to locate Kyrie Vassalos.

Until that moment she'd believed this trip had been

in vain, and that something might be wrong with her mentally to have gone this far to trace a man who didn't want to be found. But a voice inside said he still had the God-given right to know a child of his was on the way.

She'd been waiting close to an hour already. But the longer she waited, the more she expected to be told he wasn't available. If so, she would leave Egnoussa and not look back. He was a member of the Vassalos family. That was all her child needed to know.

One day years from now, it was possible Dev—or whatever he called himself—would be confronted by his son or daughter. That would all depend on whether or not her child was like Stephanie, and wanted to meet the man who'd given him or her life. Some children didn't want to know.

No matter; Stephanie planned to be the best mother in the world. She loved this baby growing inside her with all her heart and soul, and would do everything possible to give it the full, wonderful life it deserved.

After another ten minutes had passed, she couldn't sit there any longer, and decided to tell the man in reception that she would come back. The weather was beautiful, with a temperature in the mid-eighties. The island was so tiny she could walk around the port and then return. The doctor had told her mild exercise like walking would do her good and help bring her out of her depression.

As she got up to leave, the man who'd been at the desk walked into the room. "Ms. Walsh? I'm sorry I took so long. It seems Kyrie Vassalos is out of the country and won't be back in the foreseeable future. I'm sorry." He gave her back the snapshots.

So, it was just as Stephanie had thought. She would

have handed him one of her business cards from Crystal River Water Tours, where she took tourists and groups on swimming tours. But at the last second she thought better of it. For their unborn child's sake, she hoped Dev would be curious enough to find her on his own.

"Thank you for your time."

"You're welcome," he said with a smile.

After putting the pictures in her purse, she left the office and walked down the hallway to the entrance of the building. If she hurried, she'd be in time to make the next boat going back to Chios. Her trip hadn't been wasted. She'd done her duty for her child. That was all that really mattered.

She made her way through picturesque winding streets paved with slabs. En route she passed mansions and villas with tiled roofs built in the Aegean island architectural style. Dev lived in one of those mansions, but she feared she'd never see the home where he'd grown up, and they'd never share anything again.

Stephanie kept going until she arrived at the landing area, where she sat on a bench and raised her face to the sun. This island was its own paradise. Evidently the lure of scuba diving had caused Dev to leave it. Being born here, he would have been a water baby, which explained his natural prowess above and below the surface.

Was he a true playboy? Or maybe a hardworking shipping tycoon who took his pleasure on occasion where he could find it around the world, as in the Caribbean? She knew nothing about him. He might even have a wife and children.

Stephanie shuddered to think she could have been

with a married man. If that were the case, she would never forgive herself for sleeping with someone else's husband. If he had a wife, it could only hurt her to see Stephanie's business card. She was glad she hadn't left it.

Face it. You took a huge risk being with him at all.

Disturbed by her thoughts, she reached in her purse for some food to help abate her nausea. She ate a sandwich and drank some bottled water she'd brought with her. The doctor told her she needed to eat regularly, to maintain her health. For once she *was* hungry, probably because she finally knew Dev Harris was a Vassalos and could be reached here.

After finishing her sandwich, she pulled out a small bag of grapes she'd purchased in a fruit market. On impulse she offered to share them with an older woman who'd just sat down by her.

The woman smiled and took a few. "Thank you," she said in heavily accented English.

"Please take more if you like."

She nodded. "You are a tourist?"

"No. I came to visit someone, but he wasn't here."

"Ah. I wait for a friend."

"Do you live here?"

"Yes."

Stephanie's pulse raced. "Do you know the Vassalos family?"

"Who doesn't! That's one of their boats." She pointed to a beautiful white boat, probably forty-five to fifty feet long, docked in the marina. "Why do you ask?"

"It's their son I came to see."

"They have two sons. One works here. The other I never see. He's always away."

Did that mean he was always doing family business elsewhere?

Unable to sit there after that news, Stephanie got to her feet. Maybe all wasn't lost yet. "It's been very nice talking to you. Keep the grapes. I think I'll take a walk until the boat gets here."

Without wasting another second, she headed in the direction of the moored craft. Maybe one of the crew would tell her where she could reach Dev. She'd come this far....

Closer now, she realized it was a small state-of-the-art recreational yacht, the luxurious kind she occasionally spotted in Florida waters, but she saw no one around. After walking alongside, she called out, "Hello? Is anyone here?" But there was no answer.

Upon further inspection she took in the outdoor lounge with recliners and a sun bed. Beyond it was the transom, with water skis, a rope and scuba gear. The sight of the equipment brought back piercingly sweet pain.

She stepped closer and called out again. Still no answer. Since the boat that would take her back to Chios wasn't in sight yet, she decided to wait a few more minutes for someone to come.

Praying she wouldn't get caught, she sat down facing the open sea and hooked her arms around her upraised knees. Before long she spotted the boat in the distance, headed toward the harbor.

Time to go.

Her spirits reached rock bottom because she'd come to the end of her journey. With her head down, she retraced her steps along the pier. "Oh—" Stephanie cried out in surprise as a hard male body collided with hers. She felt a strong pair of hands catch her by the upper arms to prevent her from falling.

Through the wispy cotton of her white blouson top the grip felt familiar. But when she lifted her head, nothing was familiar about the narrowed pair of glittering black eyes staring into hers as if she were an alien being.

"*Dev—*"

It *was* him, but he was so changed and forbidding, she couldn't comprehend it. He released her as if she'd scorched him, and kept walking.

"Dev!" she called in utter bewilderment. "Why won't you even say hello? What's happened to you?"

He continued walking, not fast or slow, never turning around.

She thought she'd been in pain when she'd opened the box of gardenias to discover he'd gone, but this pain reached the marrow of her bones.

Let him go, Stephanie. Let it all go.

Turning away from him, she kept walking, and had almost reached the beach area when he called to her in his deep voice. "Stephanie? Come back."

She looked over her shoulder at him. "When you left the Caribbean so fast, I worried you were ill or even dying, but obviously you're fine. Don't worry. I'm leaving and won't venture near again."

"Come back, or I'll be forced to come after you."

She heard the authority in his voice that left her in no doubt he'd do exactly that. With her heart thudding, she started toward him. By the time she reached him, her khaki-clad legs would have buckled if he hadn't helped her onto the nearest padded bench aboard the yacht.

The last time she'd seen him he'd been in his bathing suit after their dive. His eyes had smoldered with desire as he'd kissed her passionately, before they'd parted to get ready for dinner. He'd told her to hurry, then had pressed another long, hot kiss to her mouth. Neither of them could bear to be separated.

Or so she'd thought.

This brooding version of Dev looked formidably gorgeous. He was wearing white cargo pants and a gray crew-necked T-shirt. His black wavy hair had grown longer, setting off the deep bronze of his complexion. With his height and fit physique, he bore the aura of a man in command, just as she and the girls had supposed. But he'd lost weight.

He lounged against the side of the boat, his hands curled around the edge, his long legs extended. *Legs he'd wrapped possessively around hers, whether under the water or in bed.* But there was a gauntness to his handsome, chiseled features that suggested great sorrow or illness. She'd been right about two things: he'd left the Caribbean on some kind of emergency, and was a native Greek down to every black hair on his head.

"I heard you showed up at the shipping office, but I never dreamed I'd find you outside the *Diomedes.* What are you doing here?"

Stephanie could hardly fathom the frigidity of his words. "I told you. After what we shared, you left so fast without an explanation I could live with, I feared something terrible must have happened to you. I—I needed to see for myself," she stammered.

"I thought the card I left with the flowers summed things up."

"It did, but I guess I'm a hard case."

She heard his sharp intake of breath. "I'll ask again. What are you doing here?"

"I came to Greece to find you, and was told you were away on business indefinitely. The man at the desk didn't give me any additional information, so I was trying to find someone on this yacht who might tell me where you were. But no one was about."

"Evidently that didn't stop you from waiting around." He spoke in a low wintry tone so unlike him she shivered in fresh pain. "In your desperation, I'm surprised you didn't come to Egnoussa much sooner."

Her desperation? What on earth was wrong? How could he have changed into a completely different person? He might not like seeing her again, but his demeanor bordered on loathing.

Though terrified at the thought he might be seriously ill, and stung by his hostile behavior, Stephanie still held her ground. "I would have been here the next day if I'd known where you lived. But the note you put with the gardenias didn't tell me where I could find you."

"How remiss of me." Coupled with his sarcasm was an icy smile, devastating her further. "Still, with the help you were given, you managed to track me down easily enough."

"If you're talking about God's help, you're right."

Evidently he didn't like her response, because he straightened to his full height. "Even knowing you as I thought I did, I have to admit I'm surprised you'd use that excuse to cover who you really are."

"Who *I* really am?" Despite being stymied, she lifted her chin proudly. "Then we're on even footing, because I don't know who you are either. The man I met in the Caribbean was named Dev Harris, an international exporter from New York on a scuba diving holiday. A man who made our dive master, Angelo, look like a beginner."

Below black brows, Dev's dark eyes pierced her to the core of her being. This frontal view of his face exposed shadows beneath them, and carved lines around his mouth that hadn't been there before. Despite her anger it grieved her that he could have been suffering all this time.

"And you made quite the seductress."

A gasp escaped her throat over the unexpected remark thrown out at her like that. Incredulous, she shook her head. "Seductress? I don't know what you're talking about."

"Come on, Stephanie. The game is over. Working for Crystal River Water Tours, you don't make the kind of money to send you all over the world, on two occasions in the last three months, without a definite agenda."

For a moment she was so shocked, she couldn't make a sound.

"However, I have to admit you played your hand with such finesse, you almost took me to the cleaners, as you Americans say. I barely got out of there in time."

"In time? For what?" She couldn't begin to understand him. In a slow rage over his indictment of her, she moved closer. "Curious you'd say that, because it seems I flew out of Providenciales too late."

He folded his powerful arms. "And now you're in

trouble up to the last silvery-gold strand of hair on your beautiful head."

"Yes," she answered in a quiet voice, without blinking. Trouble that came wrapped in a baby quilt, with a bottle of formula, among other things.

A white ring encircling his mouth gave evidence of the negative emotion fueling him. "So you're here to continue where you left off."

She swallowed hard. Two could play at this game he'd accused her of. If she could keep him talking, maybe she'd find out what was going on. He wasn't the same Dev. "Only if you still want me."

"That's an interesting proposition. Why don't you make me...*want* you." His voice grated the words. "If you can accomplish that feat, I'll let you name your price."

"What price are you talking about?" she cried in absolute shock.

His eyes narrowed to black slits. "One way or another, money is the reason *you're* here."

"You think?"

In spite of his cruelty to her, his dare emboldened Stephanie to take him up on it. Much as she wished she could turn off her desire for this man whose child she was carrying, it didn't work that way. With her only thought being to get to the bottom of this nightmare, she reached for him and slid her arms around his neck.

"I've missed you," she whispered, before pressing her mouth to his, needing to be convincing so he'd listen to her. "You have no idea how much." After three months deprivation, her longing for him was at full strength, despite her pain at being abandoned. She needed to feel his arms around her and be kissed the way he'd done before, as if he was dying for her.

At first she could wring no response from him, and couldn't bear it. Then, suddenly, she felt his groan before he pulled her closer, as if he couldn't help himself. Every remembered memory came flooding back...the rapture, the ecstasy of his mouth and hands doing incredible things to her.

If anything, the flame of heat licked at both of them even more strongly than before. She rejoiced that she'd found him and that he still wanted her. His response couldn't be feigned. He was definitely covering up something. But right this minute intense desire was the one truth between them, and she'd cling to it with every breath she possessed until she knew what had happened to him.

Their bodies swayed due to the intensity of their passion. He clung to her with surprising strength. Voluptuous warmth enveloped them, bringing her inestimable pleasure that was spiraling, taking her over the edge of coherent thought. "Could we go someplace private?" she begged against his lips. "I've needed to feel you like this for so long, but I'm afraid someone will see us."

After a slight hesitation, he tore his lips from hers and released her. Before he pulled away she thought she saw torment in his eyes. "Come with me." He sounded out of breath.

"Wait. I dropped my purse." She retrieved it from the deck floor.

"No luggage?" he asked, falling back into that accusatory tone she hated.

"I only planned to come here for a few hours, so I left it in my hotel room on Chios."

He studied her through veiled eyes, no doubt assessing the validity of her statement before grasping her hand. "We'll go below." Nikos pulled her to the top of the stairs and they descended. He led her down the hallway past the lounge. Beyond it was the galley and a laundry room. The master bedroom was on the end, with its en suite bathroom.

The bed was unmade. Had he slept on board last night? While she stood there, bombarded with questions she needed answers to, he shrugged out of his T-shirt. After throwing it on a chair, he sat on the end of the bed to remove his sandals. She took a quick breath when he stood up to get out of his cargo pants. Despite his weight loss, he was such a striking man her mouth went dry looking at his hard-muscled frame.

"What are you doing?"

He shot her a penetrating glance. "I thought this was what you wanted. I'll pay your price after we're finished. Let me help you." In a lightning move he reached for her purse and tossed it on the chair on top of his shirt, panicking her.

"Wait, Dev—"

But he was beyond listening to her. "Delightful as that blouse is, I'm aching to see you again without any artifice. It's been a long time since our all-nighter. Kissing you has caused me to remember how delightful you are. Do you want to remove it, or shall I?"

Suddenly apprehensive, she stepped away from him. The challenge she'd initiated, to break him down, had backfired and she started to be afraid. "Please don't be like this, Dev. We need to talk." She refused to tell him why she'd come all this way, until she understood the reason he'd changed into someone else. If he made love to her, he'd know what she was hiding.

His smile had a wicked curl. "I don't remember you being this coy with me before. Come here." He inched closer and caressed her cheek. "We were lovers. Why pretend to be shy now when you were—shall we say— so accommodating before?"

Heat flooded her face. He was the most irresistible male alive. She couldn't bear it that there was this awful anger emanating from him. "For one night I slept in your bed, but I wouldn't call us lovers, not when you took off the next day, never to be seen again."

She felt his hands circle her neck, where he rubbed his thumbs over the pulse throbbing in the hollow of her throat. "That must have been a shock, eh?" he taunted. "Didn't you like the flowers I left behind?" he whispered silkily. "You told me gardenias were your favorites."

Stephanie had promised herself she wouldn't break down in front of him, but she had to fight the sting of salt against her eyelids. "I loved them, and would have thanked you if you'd left me a forwarding address or phone number."

His hands slid to her hair, where his fingers curled around the strands of her ponytail. "Since you've found me anyway, come to bed and show me just how much you loved them. Don't worry. You'll get what you came for."

She shook her head. "Don't do this, Dev. Whatever terrible thing you think I've done, those ten days we spent together have to account for something to cherish."

"Cherish?" he mocked, wounding her all over again, before freeing her. His hands went to his hips in a stance of male beauty all its own. "That word connotes fidelity, loyalty. I wonder if an ounce of either quality exists inside that delectable body of yours." His response dripped like acid from his lips.

Dev would be shocked if he knew what existed inside her and was growing with every passing minute. She pressed her arms to her waist, unable to forget for one second that she was carrying his son or daughter.

"It's clear you believe I betrayed you in some way. How could I have done that? We were together constantly at the resort. On that first day you asked *me* to be your diving partner, not the other way around. I spent every waking moment with you instead of the girls who came with me. I never even left the resort to go shopping with them, because you wanted to be with me every second.

"When I read the note left in the flowers, you have no idea what it did to me. I realized I was only a spring fling to you. I—I thought it was more." Her voice caught. Feeling unexpectedly nauseous, she moved over to the bed and sank down to recover.

He pinned her with those jet-black eyes. "Yet even though you got the message that our interlude was over, you came here, anyway."

After what they'd shared, for him to say that it had been over since they'd left the Caribbean caused her spirits to plummet to a new low.

"Yes. It was important for me to see you again, to find out why you had to go back to your work so abruptly. What if you needed help? Possible reasons for your sudden disappearance plagued me, until I couldn't sleep. I feared it might have even been a medical emergency that prompted you to write me that note, and you didn't want me to worry about you.

"All this time I've wondered if something terrible had happened to you or your family, and you couldn't confide in anyone who knew you. I simply didn't know." She bit her lip. "A few days ago I couldn't stand it any longer and decided to search for you."

"How did you manage that? Who told you my name?" He sounded beyond livid.

"No one!" she cried. "At least not in the way you mean."

"Explain that to me."

She stood up again, kneading her hands together. "When I couldn't find a number or address for you in New York, I turned to the employees at the resort to try to get answers." By the time she'd explained everything she'd done, his expression looked thunderous.

His dark head flew back. "Are you telling me you figured out what plane flew me out of the Caribbean?"

"Not at first. Taking you at your word that you had an emergency at work, I thought about the flights. One to Los Angeles and one to Vancouver. Why would you go to either place when you were working in New York? The private jet to Greece made no sense, either, at least not at first.

"I spent all night wondering. By morning I looked the name up on the computer and discovered Vassalos Maritime Shipping located on the island of Egnassou. I didn't know if you were a Vassalos from Vassalos Maritime Shipping or an employee. But since you'd told me you worked for an international export company, I thought it was a close enough connection to find out.

That's why I brought the photographs, in case someone recognized you.

"I thought there might be a chance I could find you
here. When the man at the shipping office desk recognized your picture, I knew I'd come to the end of
my search. That's when I realized you'd been lying to
me the whole time. Undoubtedly, you do that whenever you meet a woman to enjoy for a time before you
disappear."

For a full minute he studied every square inch of her,
his expression lethal. "Since you've accomplished your
objective, let's go to bed for old time's sake, one more
time, shall we? Then I'll send you on your way with
enough money to have made your trip worthwhile."

Her body stiffened. "I don't want your money and
have already gotten what I came for, Dev."

"The name is Nikos, as you damn well know!"

Nikos...

Somehow she'd thought Dev would soften while
they were alone, and tell her why he'd lied to her. But
the inscrutable man facing her bore little resemblance
to her secret Adonis who'd brought her joy every second they'd been together. It hadn't mattered whether
they'd been walking on the beach or finding glorious
sights in the aqua depths of the sea.

She decided this man didn't deserve to know about
the baby until it was born. He wouldn't believe her if
she told him now, anyway. In fact, she was beginning to
think he'd drummed up this betrayal business on purpose, to get rid of her. He'd probably pulled the same
excuse on his other lovers when he was through with
them. If that was true, he'd done a stellar job.

Now that she had the main phone number of Vassalos

Shipping, she could always leave a message for him next January. If he cared to answer, he'd learn then that he was a new father, not before.

His smile was beautifully cruel. "You've been playing me for a reason. Now I want to know what it is."

Stephanie drew in a fortifying breath. "I'd hoped to get an honest answer out of you, but you're not Dev Harris. Let's just say I don't want to ruin my memory of him. You, sir, are someone I don't care to know. For all I know you have a wife and children. The thought of committing adultery with you makes me sick."

She would have reached for her purse to leave, but that's when she saw a cane resting against the wall at the side of the closet. Stephanie looked up at Dev, noticing he'd lost a little color and was braced against the door to prevent her escape.

When he'd grabbed her earlier on deck, they'd both weaved a little. She'd thought it was because the impact had caught him totally off guard, but now she knew that wasn't true. He *was* unsteady. Something serious must have happened for a man as fit as he was to need a cane. Why was he being so brutal to her? She couldn't comprehend it.

"What is it you want, if not money?"

"A little honesty. I—I feel like I'm in the middle of a nightmare." Her voice faltered.

"You're part of mine, didn't you know?" he growled. "Can you still stand there and tell me you found me through Delia's boyfriend?"

"It's the truth!"

"Surely you can do better than that." His tone stung like a whiplash.

"Dev... Nikos... Tell me what I've done?" Her cry

rang in the cabin's interior. "Are you truly so devoid of feeling that you can leave me hanging like this without one word of explanation?"

"Isn't this a case of the pot calling the kettle black?"

Stephanie had taken enough of his abuse. "Let me pass." She feared she was going to be sick.

His black brows furrowed. "You're not wanted here, but since you've shown up anyway, you're not going anywhere until I get an honest explanation."

She shook her head. "Why do you continue to accuse me of something I don't understand?"

Anger marred his arresting features. "Who told you about me? How did you know I'd be staying at that particular resort? Where did you get your information?"

"I don't know what you're talking about."

"You were obviously lying in wait for me at the resort."

"You mean like some femme fatale, so I could get you to sleep with me?"

"Were you hoping to get pregnant by a rich man? Is that it? Your latest boyfriend didn't quite live up to your dreams?"

By this time she was fuming. "Let's presume for a minute you guessed it and that was my sin. What about *your* sin? You slept with me, too."

He hunched of his broad shoulders slightly. "So I did."

"Only it seems just one night was all you wanted before you moved on. Now that I've come here, you're disgusted to see me and obviously regret our interlude." With her hair caught back in a short ponytail, and her probable lack of color, she realized she must look dreadful to him.

"But not you." His eyes had become mere slits. "Who told you about me and my family? How did you know about me?"

She couldn't believe her ears. "No one!" *Only an innocent child who doesn't have a voice yet.* "I was foolish enough to come looking for you here b-because I couldn't believe it was over between us," she stammered. That was the truth, just not all of it.

His expression remained implacable.

Stephanie averted her eyes. "It was wrong of me to sleep with you. I was raised to be wiser than that, a lesson I learned too late. But no, Dev. No matter how much you despise me for coming here uninvited, I could never regret anything so beautiful. Now I'm leaving, but I need to use your bathroom first." She was going to be sick.

CHAPTER THREE

STEPHANIE SWEPT PAST him, causing Nikos to bite down hard so hard he almost cracked a tooth. That week in the Caribbean with her had been beautiful. The most beautiful experience of his life. To think it had been a deliberate setup!

Enflamed to realize she'd used him, Nikos snatched her purse from the chair and dumped the contents on the bed, hoping to learn something. Anything!

Among the contents were three vials of pills, a wallet, a phone, a key card for the Persephone Hotel along the waterfront in Chios, an airline ticket and her passport. He examined it but saw no red flag. Her wallet gave no clues except some pictures. Two of them were of her and Nikos. Another was of her friends and still another of a woman who looked to be her mother. He also found her business card from Crystal River Water Tours.

With a grimace he reached for one of the bottles, which contained vitamins. Nikos opened it and could smell them before emptying the pills on the bed. He examined the second vial, of iron pills. The third held a prescription drug issued from the same pharmacy in Florida. Dr. Verl Sanders. Three a day as necessary for nausea and/or vomiting. The date on all three bottles indicated they'd been issued two days ago.

She was pregnant. Just as his father had intimated…

He swung his head in her direction. By now she'd come back out and was sitting on the chair. "Please, Dev." Her blue eyes begged him, out of a face with a slight pallor he hadn't noticed before. Come to think of it, with that wan complexion, she didn't look the same. The glow of health that had radiated off her in the Caribbean was missing. "If I could have one of those small greenish pills with some water?"

She still insisted on using his fictitious name. Nikos picked up one of the pills, then grasped her upper arm and led her back into his bathroom. Her firm flesh, warm from walking on the island in the sun, was a potent reminder of what he'd been torn from at the resort, but that golden quality about her had disappeared.

"Use the cup from the dispenser."

Stephanie took one and put it under the faucet. When he handed her the pill, she swallowed it with half a cup of water. He'd expected resistance, but the eager way she drank and the slight tremor of the hand holding the cup revealed a vulnerability that brought out his protective instincts and caused his mind to reel.

"How far along are you?"

The empty cup fell into the sink. This was no act. She weaved in place, causing him to tighten his grip on her arm so she wouldn't fall. Her eyes stared at him in the mirror. "You do the math."

That comment—just when he'd felt himself softening toward her—caught him on the raw. He gripped her other arm to bring her close to him, and gave her a little shake. "Whose baby is it? Rob's?"

"You can ask me that?" she cried, sounding so wounded it almost got to him.

"Very easily."

Her head fell back on the slender column of her neck. "Rob? The guy I only had one dinner date with? I was never intimate with him or anyone else! I can't believe you brought his name up."

"I used protection, Stephanie."

"That's what I told Dr. Sanders. He said no protection was perfect, and informed me I was going to have a baby. I'm three months along."

She'd already gone through her first trimester? He'd been in absolute hell during that same time period.

"Call him and he'll confirm it. If you can conceive of my being with another man after what we shared on vacation, then your imagination is greater than mine could ever be. After it's born and you're still in doubt, then a simple DNA test will tell you the truth."

The blood hammered in his ears. He searched her eyes, trying to find any trace of duplicity in her, but could see none. His lips twisted. "So your carefully laid plan had the consequence you'd hoped for, and now you're ready to turn this to your advantage?"

"What advantage?" she blurted angrily. "When you were through with me, you sent me flowers and couldn't have made it clearer our interlude was over. But I happen to believe that a man who's a womanizer still deserves to know he's going to be a father. That's the real reason I'm here!"

The *real* reason. *Which truth was the truth?*

"I could have sent you a bouquet with a note congratulating you on your new status. But I had no idea where to send it, so I decided to do the decent thing and come in person, hoping to find Dev Harris. Instead I found *you*."

With her wintry indictment, she jerked herself out of his arms and hurried back to the bedroom. "Now that you've been given the news, I need to catch the boat back to Chios." She started to put the contents of her purse back, but his hand was faster, preventing her.

"I'm afraid not. There won't be another one until tomorrow." He slid her cell phone and passport in a pocket of his pants.

Her head swerved to meet his piercing gaze. "I never wanted or expected anything from you, and that's a good thing, because I don't know who you are."

"Nor I you." His voice grated. "Except in the biblical sense." He saw a glint of pain in her eyes before she started for the doorway. "Go ahead, but without a passport, you won't be allowed to board the plane back to the States."

"You can't keep me here! I have a job to get back to, a condo to take care of. My flight leaves for Florida in the morning."

"You should have thought of that before you ever targeted me."

Her naturally arched brows frowned in puzzlement. "You certainly have an inflated opinion of yourself. I've met men in Florida with a lot of money. Maybe not as much as the Vassalos family, but enough to keep a grasping woman in style for the rest of her life. Since you can't wait for me to be gone, how long do you intend to keep me here?"

"For as long as it takes to get the truth from you."

She sat down on the edge of the bed as if she was too weak to stand. Her pallor convinced him that part of her story was the truth. She was nauseous, but maybe it covered something other than pregnancy. Kon's wife had done a spectacular job of convincing him she was pregnant.

"Dev... We met purely by accident, when I was scuba diving at the resort with my friends from Crystal River."

"Yet you managed to locate me here without any difficulty whatsoever. Now you're telling me you're pregnant with my child. We both know you were already pregnant when you slept with me on vacation. If you're hoping to inveigle your way into my life with this announcement, it won't work."

By now her hands had formed into fists, and she jumped up from the bed. "I don't want to stay here!" she cried, sounding on the verge of hysteria. "I can't! I'm expected back at work. My friends will wonder where I am."

He would never have credited her with being an hysterical woman. It didn't fit with what he knew about her. Yet what did he really know, except what she'd allowed him to see while they were both on vacation? "No problem. You can call them and tell them you've been detained."

"Dev—"

"It's Nikos, remember?"

"All right then. Nikos. Please don't do this. I need to get back to the hotel in Chios for my personal belongings."

"We'll sail there and Yannis will collect them for you."

"Yannis?"

"He's a seaman who worked for my family when I was boy. Now he works for me."

"What do you mean, collect?" she asked in fresh alarm.

"After we leave Chios, we won't be touching land again for at least two weeks."

After letting out a moan, she started pacing, then stopped. "Call my obstetrician in Florida. He'll verify the dates so you'll have your proof."

"That won't prove anything. You could have been with a man the night before we met. Maybe several."

A gasp escaped. "Surely you don't believe that! There was only you. Phone Delia. She'll verify everything."

"How much did you pay her and her boyfriend to tell me a lie if I called her?"

Stephanie paled more. "Nikos...who are you?"

He raked a hand through his hair, wondering the same thing. After living through a hellish childhood with his father, plus the memory of Kon's disastrous marriage and divorce, Nikos had developed a much more cynical outlook on life.

Part of him couldn't help but wonder why Natasa had been waiting around for him all these years, if not to marry money. She'd lived with wealth all her life and needed a rich husband to be kept in that same lifestyle. The thought sickened him.

What if Stephanie was telling him the truth? His black brows furrowed. "Someone who doesn't like being taken advantage of. You were very clever to try and convince me you found me by sheer perseverance. For the time being you'll remain with me on the *Diomedes.*" It was an impulsive decision, one he hadn't had time to examine yet.

She looked frantic. "Please don't do this."

For a moment he was carried back three months in time. She'd begged him not to tease her when he kept kissing her face, but not her mouth. He'd been on the verge of devouring her and couldn't hold back much longer. Just now that same appeal was in her voice, confusing him, when he needed to keep his wits.

"You don't have to worry. I'll let you contact your boss and make it right with him. Tell him your medical condition has made it necessary for you to stay in Greece for an indefinite period. Your boss will have to understand."

"But Nikos—"

"No doubt your friend Melinda will run by your condo for you and check your mail." He put his T-shirt back on and slid into his sandals. "As for you, I'll make sure you're taken care of in your fragile state. Just be grateful I'm not turning you over to the authorities for trespassing on private property. You wouldn't last long in one of our jails."

Her appealing body shuddered.

"It would be interesting to know who told you I was on the yacht. No one knows except my parents."

"I—I met an older woman waiting for the boat that would take me back to Chios," Stephanie stammered. "She pointed to this yacht and said it belonged to the Vassalos family."

"Why would she do that?"

"Because I asked her if she lived here and knew your family."

"What did she say?"

"That everyone knew your family."

"Did you exchange names?"

"No! I simply offered her some of my grapes while we were waiting for the boat."

"So at that point you just decided to walk over to the yacht and see if it met your high expectations, did you?"

"No. My intention was to find out if anyone on board knew where you really were."

"I guess I'm not surprised you decided to use your beauty to sweet-talk the crew into revealing my whereabouts."

She stiffened. "There *was* no crew."

"Yet having been told I was out of the country indefinitely, you still waited for someone to come to the yacht."

She moistened her lips. "I was afraid that if you were at work and knew I was looking for you, you'd pretend to be away. It was my last resort to try and reach you."

"Therefore once again it was pure luck that you didn't take no for an answer and sought me out at the yacht."

"It appears that way," she whispered.

"I'm afraid your luck has run out." Before he walked out of the bedroom, he said, "Go ahead and fix your own meal. There's food and drink in the galley. We just restocked everything. You're paler and weaker than I remember. That couldn't be good for you in your condition."

"I notice you've lost weight and don't look as well, either!"

Touché.

"In fact, you—" Suddenly, she stopped talking.

"I what?" he demanded.

Stephanie averted her eyes. "Nothing."

He'd seen her glance at the cane, and had an idea what she'd intended to say. It angered him further. "Don't try to go up on deck while we're leaving port."

Adrenaline drove him out of the room and down the hall to the stairs. But he paid the price for not taking care because when he reached the top deck, he felt pain at the base of his spine and realized he'd exerted himself too much without support. *Damn it all.*

CHAPTER FOUR

AFTER A FEW minutes of enforced solitude, Stephanie could feel the yacht moving. Good heavens! Nikos had really meant it. They were leaving the port and she was his prisoner! It certainly wasn't because he was enamored of her. She'd changed physically since they'd been together, making her less attractive.

His looks had altered, too, but in his case the weight loss and dark brooding behavior didn't detract from his virulent male charisma. If anything, those changes made him even more appealing, if that was at all possible.

By now she'd passed the stage where she still believed she was having a nightmare. Rage and bewilderment had been warring inside her, but her greatest need at the moment was for food, so she wouldn't throw up again. No matter what was going to happen, she needed to take care of herself and her baby.

Taking him at his word, she walked to the galley. He'd stocked his fridge well in a kitchen that rivaled that of even the most rich and famous yacht owners. Anything she could want was here. But after she'd eaten, she started going crazy with nothing to do, and decided to go up to the top of the stairs for some fresh air.

To her dismay the tough-looking seaman, Yannis, probably in his sixties, barred her way. "Go back down, Ms. Walsh," he told her in a heavily accented voice.

"Just let me stand here for a little while and breathe some fresh air." There was no sign of her baby's father. The sun had fallen below the horizon.

"Nikos doesn't want you up here until we're out on open water. It's for your safety. I promised him that I would take care of you."

There'd be no point in begging his guard dog to let her walk around on deck. "All right." She turned around and went back to the dimly lit passage below, and finally Nikos's bedroom. Stephanie couldn't believe this was the same man she'd fallen madly in love with.

Since he wasn't working at Vassalos Shipping right now, what was he doing on this yacht? Needing to figure out why he was being so cruel and secretive, she opened his closet, but all she found were casual clothes. Nothing that told her anything. The clothes in the dresser didn't reveal anything, either.

Needing answers, she left the bedroom and went along the passageway to the next door, on the left. It was another bedroom, with a queen-size bed and its own bathroom.

She tried the next door, but it was locked. Maybe it was the bedroom of the man who was crewing for Nikos. Stephanie's gaze darted to the lounge across from it. One end contained a couch, table and chairs, and an entertainment center. The other end had been made into a den, equipped with a computer and everything that went with it.

After checking out his desk, she came across sets of

maps and charts with Greek words she couldn't read. Stephanie was afraid she'd be caught snooping and it would intensify his anger. Quickly, she put them back in the drawers and hurried down the corridor to his bedroom.

Once she'd shut the door, she leaned against it with a pounding heart while her mind tried to make sense of what he was doing on the yacht. When she'd calmed down, she was so exhausted she stretched out on the bed. In case he came to check up on her, he would think she'd been sleeping instead of exploring the yacht without his permission.

Emotionally spent, she closed her eyes for a minute, trying desperately to put all the disjointed pieces together. The man at the reception desk had told her Kyrie Vassalos was out of the country and wouldn't be back in the foreseeable future. It was a blatant lie, since Nikos had obviously been living on this yacht for some time. Why?

Stephanie racked her brain for answers until she knew nothing else. When she next became aware of her surroundings, the yacht was still moving. To her surprise Nikos had thrown a blanket over her. How long had she slept? Her watch said it was 11:00 p.m., Greek time.

When she rolled over to get up, she realized he'd removed her sandals. At the end of the bed she saw her suitcase. That meant he'd already sailed to Chios, and had no doubt taken care of her hotel bill.

She started to tremble. No one in the world knew where she was right now. No one would be looking for her yet. Stephanie was being held against her will in the middle of the Aegean Sea by a man she didn't begin to know.

After slipping on her sandals, she left the bedroom and walked down the hall to the stairs. No one met her at the top. She walked to the railing and looked all around. Night had descended. In the distance she could see lights twinkling from land far away. Though the sight was beautiful, she shivered to think she'd been so foolish as to climb aboard the boat of a perfect stranger. In Greek waters, no less...

Didn't Greek mythology tell of Pandora, the first woman on earth? Zeus had given her a beautiful container with instructions not to open it under any circumstances. But her curiosity had prevailed and she did open it, letting out all the evil held inside. For what she'd done, she'd feared Zeus's wrath.

Another shudder rocked Stephanie's body. Today she'd opened that container, knowing she shouldn't have. The action had seemed so small at the time. But what she'd done, in order to find the father of her baby, had turned out to have severe and far-reaching consequences for her, inciting Nikos's wrath.

"You're not supposed to be up here."

At the sound of Nikos's deep voice, a cry escaped her lips and she spun around. The warm night breeze flattened the T-shirt against his well-defined chest, ruffling his black wavy hair. Despite his hostility, his male beauty captivated her.

"I was looking for you."

"It's dangerous to walk around at this time of night. You're lucky I didn't set the wireless security system yet, or you would have received the fright of your life by the noise."

Her hand clutched the railing. "I'm used to being on boats," she said defensively.

His lips tightened into a thin line. "Go back down. *Now.*"

Nikos's mood was too dark and ominous for her to dare defy him. Taking a deep breath, she turned around and walked back to the stairs, which she descended. She felt him following her, all the way to the bedroom.

After he came inside, she looked at him. "Was the alarm set this afternoon while I was waiting to talk to a crew member?"

"Yes, even if that part of the marina is Vassalos private property. There are some people who will trespass no matter what."

She lifted a hand to her throat. She'd considered going on board, but had held back, thank goodness. "You mean all those other boats belong to your company?"

"That's right." His chiseled features stood out in stark relief. "I must admit I'm surprised you didn't step on the *Diomedes* without permission. When we were together on Providenciales, I noticed what an adventurous person you were, unafraid to explore the depths where the others held back. I guess it doesn't really surprise me you would show such tenacity in trying to find me, regardless of the consequences."

Her softly rounded chin lifted. "That's because I was on a sacred mission."

"Sacred?" he queried silkily. "What an interesting choice of words."

Salty tears stung her eyelids. "You wouldn't understand."

"Try me."

Stephanie shook her head. "You'll only mock me, so there's no point."

"You're trying my patience, what little I have left," he said, his voice grating. He lounged against the closed door. The stance looked familiar, but she had an idea he needed the support. Stephanie wished she didn't care about his condition, but the signs of his suffering, both physical and emotional, had gotten to her. "I'm waiting."

"When we were in the Caribbean, you asked me about my father. I told you he and my mother never married and she raised me alone. But I never went into the details."

"Why was that?"

She sank down on the side of the bed. "Because it's such a painful subject for me to talk about, and because I barely knew you. Eventually I would have told you everything, but we ran out of time." Her voice shook.

His jaw hardened. "That must have been a shock to your carefully laid plans."

"I didn't have any plans, Nikos. I don't know why you won't believe me. You say you want answers, so I'm trying to give them to you. Mom met my father on a winter skiing holiday in Colorado. They spent a glorious week together before he said he had to leave, but would fly to Crystal River to see her.

"She worked in hospital administration. He could have found her at any time, but he never called or looked her up. Mom had her pride and waited in vain for him to get in touch with her."

Nikos eyed Stephanie skeptically. "If she knew where he lived, why didn't she seek him out?"

"By the time I was born, she was so ashamed of

what she'd done, she made up her mind that I would never know his name or where I could find him. She felt he didn't deserve to know he was a father. I was put in day care and she raised me with the help of my grandparents until they passed on."

Struggling with the rest, Stephanie sprang to her feet. "Since you left me at the resort, I have a crystal-clear understanding of what my mother went through and why she was so shattered. But she forgot one thing. She didn't realize how important it was for me to know who my father was, if only to see him once and understand my own genes, to gain more of an identity."

Stephanie heard Nikos take an extra breath in reaction.

"Mother robbed me of that. It's the only thing in our lives that caused pain between us. I loved her. Though she was the best mom in the world, I had a hard time forgiving her for that. However, I finally have. Still, her omission has left scars, because I'm my father's flesh and blood, too. When she died, her secret died with her, leaving me in agony and always wondering about him.

"Do I have grandparents who are still alive? A half brother or sister? Does my father like doing the things I like? Do I look like him? Those are questions for which I have no answers. Unfortunately, I'll never be given them."

She clutched her arms to her waist. "Such is the story of the Walsh mother and daughter. We were both open to a good time, until it was over. I can't believe I've repeated my mother's history, but they say experience is the best teacher."

Stephanie threw her head back. "How I've learned! I had to believe it when the doctor told me I was pregnant. He said a good condom hardly ever fails, but it can slip. That's probably what happened with us."

By now Niko's countenance had grown dark and lined.

"Believe it or not, my very first thought when I learned of my pregnancy wasn't about you or money, but about the life we'd created. I felt all the joy of being told I was going to be a mother, and I loved my baby instantly.

"But I have to tell you, I damned myself and you for the weakness that caused us to reach out for pleasure without marriage or commitment of any kind, without really knowing the most basic things about each other. We were both incredibly selfish, Nikos."

"You're right," he admitted, with what sounded like self-loathing.

"In hindsight I realize I don't hate you for what you did, leaving without a personal goodbye. I took a risk with you. We were equal partners in doing what we did. That's why I did everything I could to find you and let you know you're going to be a father. To *not* tell you would be an even more selfish act.

"I wouldn't be honest if I didn't admit that I wanted to be with you the moment we met in the Caribbean, and I made no secret about it. That time was beautiful beyond belief and something I will always treasure. It's the reason I don't want to make something ugly out of something that was sacred to me at the time, even if it was illicit. I still don't know if you have a wife or other children."

"I don't," he whispered in a bleak tone.

"If that's the truth, then I'm glad I don't have to carry that burden, too. You've accused me of coming after you because of the great Vassalos fortune. Let me say now that I wouldn't ask for money or take it under any circumstances. What we had together wasn't love. It couldn't have been, since it was based on a lie."

At her comment his features hardened.

"You owe me nothing, Nikos, but you have the right to know we're going to have a child. When the baby's born, I plan to give it the last name of Walsh. But I did want to be able to tell our daughter or son your true name—that it wasn't Dev Harris, and that you come from a fine established family from Egnoussa, Greece, and not New York.

"That's why I did everything possible to find you and learn your true identity. I realize I've gone where angels fear to tread, even to trying to find out about you from someone working on your yacht. But I've done it for our child, who doesn't deserve such selfish parents."

"It's very noble of you to take on partial blame." But his mocking tone robbed the sentiment of any meaning.

"Once you let me off this luxury vessel, I'm going back to Crystal River, knowing I've done my best for my baby. One day, when our child asks about you, I'll tell him or her all I know and learned about you during those ten days we spent together. They were the happiest days of my whole life.

"It will help satisfy our child's great need to know about his or her beginnings. Every human born wants to know who they are and where they come from. Were they wanted? I want our child to know he or she was wanted from the second I found out that I was pregnant. Once grown, it will be up to him or her if you meet. I'll play no part in it.

"Now if you'll excuse me, I need to use the bathroom again. After I've gotten ready for bed, where do you want me to sleep?"

"Your bedroom is the next one down the hallway, on the left. I'll show you. You can freshen up in your own bathroom."

He picked up her suitcase and took it to the guest bedroom she'd looked in before. "Get a good night's sleep. It appears you need it," he muttered. The unflattering observation shook her to the foundations.

Nikos had told Yannis to drop anchor off Oinoussa Island for the night. Afraid to go below and fall asleep, where he might have one of his flashbacks and Stephanie would hear him, he opted for a lounger beneath the stars, and covered himself with a light blanket.

All was quiet except for the frantic pounding of his heart at every pulse point of his body.

For the rest of the hours before dawn he lay there in torment, going over their conversation in his mind.

Even if he'd used her while on vacation, Stephanie had claimed she wanted him to know in person that he was going to be a father. At the heartbreaking story of having all knowledge of her own father kept from her, Nikos had been moved beyond words.

To go to so much trouble and expense to find Dev Harris—to risk her health in the process—led him to believe she must be telling him the truth. Otherwise she would have sought out the other man she'd been with, *if* there was another man.

But if she'd been with another man before Nikos, no one had proof of paternity. Only a blood test after the baby was born would prove it. Any earlier attempt would be a risk to the unborn baby and possibly cause a miscarriage. He didn't dare insist on it. Much as he wanted to believe he was the father, and that her true reason for coming to Greece was to inform him of the fact, he was still riddled with doubts.

Nikos closed his eyes tightly. When Kon had been confronted with a similar situation, before they'd gone into the military, he'd believed the nineteen-year-old girl who'd told him she was pregnant. Kon had gotten in over his head with an attractive French girl he'd met on vacation in Corsica, but before returning home, he realized he wasn't in love, and had ended it with her while they were still together.

To his chagrin, she'd showed up a month later with a positive result on a home pregnancy test, claiming he was the father. She was terrified of having her parents find out. What should she do?

Kon was an honorable man and had been willing to take responsibility, so they got married privately at the local church, where Nikos stood as one of the witnesses. His parents accepted her into the family and they'd lived with them until Kon could afford to find a place for them to live on their own.

But two months later his friend realized she'd lied to him and there was no baby. He got medical proof from the doctor at the hospital. She was forced to admit she'd made up the fabrication because she loved him and didn't want to lose him. If he thought they were going to have a baby, then they could get married. As it turned out her plan had worked...for a while.

Betrayed to the point he couldn't look at her anymore, he divorced her and put the whole ghastly affair behind him. But there'd been a heavy emotional price to pay, and the divorce had cost him a great deal of money, which Nikos insisted on funding from his own savings account. It was the least he could do for his friend.

After the agony Nikos had seen Kon go through when he'd realized he'd been deceived, the possibility that Stephanie was lying, too, gutted him. He didn't honestly know what to believe.

Short of making love to Stephanie to learn if she was truly pregnant, which wasn't a viable option for too many reasons to consider right now, he could phone her doctor. Yet somehow that idea was repugnant to him.

The only sure thing to do was wait for physical signs of her pregnancy. In order to do that, he would have to keep her close for the time being.

When Nikos thought back to their first meeting, he recalled he'd been the aggressor. Unlike her friends, who worked at a local hotel in Crystal River, Stephanie had done nothing to come on to him. While they'd flirted with him, she'd kept her distance and been totally serious about diving.

It turned out they didn't have her skills and snorkeled only part of each day. Oftentimes they preferred to laze on the beach and go shopping in town. Not Stephanie. Quite the opposite, in fact, which was why he'd asked her if she'd be willing to be his diving partner for the duration. He'd felt her reluctance when she'd said yes, but it was obvious she loved the sport and couldn't go diving without a partner.

Scuba diving wasn't for everyone, but she was a natural. Together they'd experienced the euphoria of discovering the underwater world. Besides her beauty, there was an instant connection between them as they'd signaled each other to look at the wonders exploding with color and life around each gully and crevice.

When they'd had to surface, he hadn't wanted it to end, and had asked her to eat dinner with him. She'd turned down his first invitation, but the second time she'd agreed. That's when he'd learned she'd grown up along Florida's Nature Coast. She'd learned to scuba dive early with her mother. After college she'd gone to work for a water tour company that took tourists scalloping and swimming with the manatees. It explained her prowess beneath the waves.

If he was truly the only man she'd been with, then her news represented a miracle. Nikos was sterile now, the hope of ever having a child from his own body having gone up in flames during the explosion.

Yet he could feel no joy if she'd set him up—no elation that a deceitful woman would be the mother of his child. If indeed he was the father...

But what if you are, Vassalos?

Think about it.

Your own flesh and blood could be growing inside Stephanie. The only son or daughter you'll ever have.

More thoughts bombarded him.

After his last mission he'd hoped to resign his commission and go after her, marry her. What if she truly was innocent of every charge, and he'd totally misread the situation? If that was the case, then one misstep on his part could hurt her emotionally and damage any chance at real happiness, with their baby on the way.

He got up from the lounger and walked over to the railing, watching the moonlight on the water. His training as a SEAL had taught him that you had to set up your perimeter and have everything in place before you mounted an assault. This time Stephanie was the target. Unfortunately, after leaving her behind, he'd unwittingly planted an almost impenetrable field of land mines and booby traps that would destroy him if he wasn't careful.

If his suspicions about her were correct—that she'd calculated every move since meeting him at the resort, in order to trap him—it meant maneuvering through them with surgical precision while he waited to see if she was pregnant, then awaited the DNA results.

How would he begin making it up to her if he was wrong?

In retrospect, Nikos realized he'd accused her of duplicity, when he'd been the one who'd committed a multiple number of sins. Not only had he forsaken her on the island without giving her an honest explanation, he hadn't tried to reach her during his stay in the hospital.

The moment his father had handed him those snapshots, Nikos had been carried away by his own suspicions that she was after his money and the lifestyle he could provide her. His anger had quickly turned to white-hot pain at the thought she'd been only using him during that time on vacation. In retaliation, he'd treated her abominably.

Nikos let out a groan. Was he turning into his father? A man who'd believed the worst about the wife who loved him, because of a rumor? Whose doubts and suspicions had turned him into an impossible man to live with, catching Nikos in the crossfire?

Stephanie's words still rang in his ears. *What we had together wasn't love.*

But what if it *had* been love on her part, and it was

only her anger talking now? Otherwise why would she have gone through all she'd done to find him?

He owed it to both of them to discover the truth. Otherwise he might be dooming himself to repeat his father's history. Until Nikos had proof, he decided he would believe her story, because his entire happiness could depend on it.

By the time the sun had risen above the horizon, he'd made his plans. The first thing he'd do was shower, then fix breakfast for the two of them. *Or the three...*

A knock on her bedroom door brought Stephanie awake. It was ten after eight. She'd slept soundly, likely because of the gentle rocking of the yacht. But it didn't feel as if they were moving now.

"Yes?"

"Your breakfast is waiting for you in the lounge down the hall, whenever you're ready."

She blinked. "Nikos?"

"Of course."

There was no "of course" about it. Last night he'd told her to fix her own food. This morning it seemed he'd decided to be more civil. That was a good sign, since she needed to go home today, and couldn't without his cooperation.

"Thank you. I'll be right there."

She took all her pills with a cup of water she'd put by the bed, and then got out from under the covers. Once in the bathroom she showered quickly, then brushed her hair and left it loose. A little blusher and lipstick and she felt ready to face Nikos.

Stephanie hadn't packed a lot. She'd brought extra undergarments and a smoky-blue knit top she wore loose over her khaki pants, which were uncomfortable now. She needed to buy some maternity clothes the moment she got back to Florida.

In spite of the fact that she would have to go through the entire pregnancy alone, she was looking forward to it. Having found the baby's father, and knowing his real identity, she felt a bit more lighthearted. Soon she'd start getting a nursery ready, and couldn't wait.

After putting on her sandals, she left the bedroom and moved across the hall to the lounge, where she found Nikos at the table, waiting for her. He stood up when she walked in. She detected the scent of the soap he'd used in the shower. Her senses responded to it, though she tried to ignore them.

"It looks like you've made a fabulous breakfast." He'd fixed coffee, too, but so far she hadn't been able to tolerate it. "We could have eaten in the galley and saved you the extra trouble."

"True, but you're a guest, so I thought this might be more enjoyable."

"For a prisoner who has to stay below deck, you mean," she muttered.

He ignored her comment. "Let's hope there's something here that you can keep down." He helped her into a chair before he sat opposite her at the rectangular table.

"Those rolls and fruit look good." So did he…. This morning he was freshly shaved and wearing a white crew neck shirt with jeans. It was sinful how handsome he was!

While he ate eggs and a roll, his jet-black eyes played over her several times. "Your hair is a little longer."

"So's yours." But she refused to tell him how much she liked it.

He appeared to drink his coffee with pleasure. "What did your doctor tell you about swimming and scuba diving in your condition?"

The question was totally unexpected. "I can do some limited swimming, but diving during pregnancy increases the risk to the fetus, so I'm not taking any chances. Why do you ask?"

One black brow lifted. "Your job. Now that you're pregnant, the kind of work you do swimming with the manatees will have to be curtailed."

She munched on a banana. "I realize that and plan to discuss it with my boss when I get back. Which raises the question of when you're going to take me to Chios so I can get a flight home."

"That all depends." He bit into a juicy plum.

Stephanie fought to remain cool-headed. "On what?"

He finished it, then lounged back in the chair, eyeing her for a long moment. "I have a proposition for you."

"I'm not interested."

"Surely after all the trouble you took to find me, can't you admit you're a little curious?"

"That curiosity died when I didn't find Dev. You're the dark side of him, a complete stranger to me with your lies and secrets. I have no desire to listen to anything you have to say, except to hear that you'll let me go."

"Be that as it may, you've convinced me you were an innocent tourist on vacation in the Caribbean. I take full responsibility for finding you attractive and pursuing you. Since you're pregnant, it's only right that I take care of you and the baby you're carrying."

For him to say that to her now... Pain ripped her apart. "For the last time, I don't want your money, just my freedom."

His eyes narrowed on her features. "You can have it in time *if* it's what you want. That's what divorces are for."

Shaken by his words, she sprang from the chair. "What are you talking about?"

"Our marriage, of course. You came all the way from Florida to let me know I'm going to be a father. But that's not all I want. I want my name on the birth certificate along with yours. To a Greek male, it means everything."

"Since when?" she blurted.

"Since learning that you've known nothing about your own father—not even his name. I can see how devastating that has been for you, which makes it more vital than ever that the baby growing inside you has my name so it can take its rightful place in the world."

Stephanie reeled in place, clinging to the back of the chair. "You don't want to marry me." Her tremulous words reverberated in the lounge.

Now Nikos was on his feet. "On the contrary. It's all I thought about during the night."

"Why?" she cried in torment.

"Because this baby is already precious to me."

Her anger flared. "Last night you questioned if it was even yours."

"Last night I was in denial that a miracle had happened."

She shook her head. "What do you mean?"

"A lot has occurred since we last saw each other."
He didn't need to tell her that. Her whole world had
been turned upside down. "I was in a boating accident
that landed me in the hospital with a spinal injury."

Stephanie bit her lip, pained by the news. "I knew
something was wrong," she whispered. "Sometimes
you're a little unsteady. I noticed it wh-when you were
holding me."

"Nothing gets past you, does it? Your unexpected
presence on the *Diomedes* gave me away. Fortunately,
I'm getting stronger every day and use the cane only
when I'm tired. But I'm not the man I once was and
never will be. Furthermore, the accident had certain
repercussions I can't do anything about."

Her mouth went dry. She was almost afraid to hear.
"What are they?"

"For one thing, my injury left me sterile."
Sterile?

A slight gasp escaped her lips, for she knew that
kind of news had to be soul wrenching to a man.
"Surely it's only a temporary setback?"

"No." His eyes again narrowed to slits. "It's permanent." The throb in his voice carried its own haunt-
ing tale.

Stephanie pressed her hand to her mouth to stifle her
cry. "I'm so sorry, Nikos. I hardly know what to say."

"Perhaps now you understand why your coming
here to tell me you're pregnant, at the very moment
I've been dealing with my news, made me go out of
my head for a little while. After having to give up all
hope of having my own child, I suppose I was afraid
to believe you were telling me the truth."

Stephanie's lungs tightened while she tried to absorb

the revelation. "What was the other repercussion?" She feared it was going to be horrible, too.

"My best friend died in the accident."

"Kon Gregerov?"

Nikos nodded gravely.

"Oh, no..." She couldn't hold back the tears. They rolled down her cheeks. He'd mentioned his friend several times while they'd been diving. He'd told her they were closer than he was to his own brother. They'd grown up together and would have done anything for each other.

After such trauma, was it any wonder he'd changed so completely in every way? Other than anger over what life had dealt him, Nikos had to feel dead inside. If their positions were reversed, Stephanie knew her life would look black to her.

"Now that you've heard the truth from me, here's my proposition. I want to marry you as soon as possible, and we'll live here. It will mean having to give up your job. You can either sell or rent your condo, and put your car and furnishings in storage for the time being.

"It's the only way I can protect you and the baby. But it wouldn't have been fair to you if I hadn't told you I can't give you more children. Millions of other men can. You need to think about that very carefully before you commit yourself legally to me."

Stephanie *was* thinking. It was a shock that she was going to have a baby at all. Right now she couldn't contemplate having more children. Though she knew Nikos wasn't in love with her, she had proof he'd been deadly honest with her just now. Knowing the only child he would ever have was on the way might give him a reason to go on living.

But there was a part of him that didn't know if he was the father or not. And she had concerns, too, if a marriage between them was going to take place. She knew so little about him.

"Nikos?" She wiped the moisture off her face. "What is it you do for a living?"

He put his hands in his back pockets. "I used to work for the family shipping business. Now I'm in the process of starting up something new with Kon's elder brother. It's a project we used to talk about a lot."

"What's his name?"

"Tassos. He's a good friend, too, and married, with a child."

"Does it have to do with shipping?"

"No. We're planning to drill for natural gas in this part of the Aegean."

She knew Nikos was extraordinary, but to consider such an undertaking meant he was a man with vision. It took away her fear that he may have lost interest in everything, including life. To know he was working on something so vital for his own well-being, not to mention his country, thrilled her. Suddenly all those maps and charts she'd seen in the desk made sense.

"You don't need to worry that I can't take care of you," he said mockingly.

"Don't be absurd. The thought never crossed my mind. Nikos? Have you ever been married?"

A caustic laugh escaped. "No, although my family has had a girl picked out for me for years now."

Someone he loved? "You mean a beautiful, well-heeled Greek woman of a good family from your social class. Until I showed up yesterday, were you planning to marry her?"

"No. Natasa wants children. That's the one thing I can't give her."

But he's given one to me, his only one. Stephanie's heart rejoiced, despite the fact she knew he wasn't in love with her.

"When the news gets out that you and I are married, she'll have to move on," he muttered.

Nikos hadn't answered her question, but it didn't matter. Having another woman waiting at home, approved of by his family, explained why he'd never made a commitment to Stephanie on the island. She had enough charity in her heart to feel sorry for Natasa. Nikos was a prize who stood out from every male she'd ever met.

"If I were to agree to marry you, I wouldn't want a big wedding, Nikos."

"That's one area we fully agree on. We'll have it take place in private, with only Yannis and the Gregerov family as witnesses."

Alarmed, she turned to him. "Not even your parents?"

"Especially not them." Stephanie cringed, there was so much heat behind his declaration. "My father and I have been at odds for a long time."

"Your mother, too?"

"Let's just say she's loyal to my father and takes his part in most everything, to keep things civil."

That's why Nikos had never spoken of them on vacation. What could have happened to cause such a breach? "I'm sorry."

He eyed her soulfully. "No more sorry than I am for you to have lived with the hurt your mother inflicted, even if she did it for what she believed were the right reasons. My father justifies his decisions in the same way, without considering the damage. You and I share a common bond in that regard."

A world of hurt laced his words.

"After we're married, we'll drop by the house for a visit and tell them. They'll come around after the baby's born. My parents want grandchildren."

Stephanie eyed him carefully. "Do they know that the accident made you s-sterile?" she stammered.

Frown lines marred his face. "No. To them, children are everything. I don't ever want them to know."

She could understand that. If his family pitied him, he'd never be able to handle it. Stephanie was coming to find out what a private person he was. "Have you considered how they'll feel about me when we're introduced? I'm afraid they'll never see a pregnant American woman from a single family, with no father in the picture, as worthy to be your wife."

His features hardened. "You're carrying a Vassalos inside your body. That makes you the worthiest of all."

Her baby was a Walsh, too, but Nikos had his pride, and right now she knew he was clinging to that one bright hope. More than ever Stephanie realized he was planning on the baby being his. Otherwise there'd be no visit to his family, and her marriage to Nikos would be dissolved.

In order to put him out of his pain, she could swear on the Bible that he was the father, so he'd be reassured, but it would do no good. He needed proof.

Last night he'd told her to go below. She'd thought he was just being mean-spirited, because he was angry. But hearing about the boating accident that had cost his friend his life made her realize Nikos was being protective.

He'd been that way with her scuba diving, always watching out for her. It was his nature. She'd found that trait in him particularly reassuring and remarkable, but she still had reservations about marrying him.

"Earlier you mentioned divorce."

"That's because we don't know what the future will bring after the baby is born."

"You mean you might not want to live with me any-more, under the same roof."

He cocked his head. "As I recall, you were the one who said that what we had on vacation wasn't love. I'm just trying to cover every contingency so there won't be any more surprises. I'd say we've both had enough of them since we met in the Caribbean, and need to lay the groundwork if this is going to work."

Pragmatic was the operative word. She could hardly breathe. "Where would we live?"

"Because of my work with Tassos, I prefer the yacht for the time being. We'll dock at various ports so you can go ashore and explore. A little later on I'll buy us a villa on Oinoussa Island, near the Gregerov's, where you can set up a nursery. Tassos's wife, Elianna, and his younger sister, Ariadne, both had babies recently and speak excellent English. They're warm and friendly. You'll like them."

"I'm sure they're very nice."

The problem was, Stephanie didn't speak any Greek. Yesterday she hadn't known if Dev was even in Eg-noussa. Last evening he'd turned into Nikos Vassalos; today he was talking marriage to her. But he wasn't the man she'd fallen headlong in love with on vacation.

That time with Dev could never be recaptured, and she found herself grieving all over again.

Unfortunately, she didn't have the luxury of shedding more tears. For the sake of their child, it was Nikos, not Dev, who'd proposed to her, in order to give their baby a legitimate name and legacy.

"Any more questions?"

"I'm sure more will come up, but right now I can't think of any." She clutched the chair railing. "Is there anything else important you haven't confided to me?"

He rubbed the side of his jaw. "Yes. If you agree to marry me, then I'll tell you the rest. But if you would prefer that I set you up on Oinoussa as my pillow friend and a kept woman, so I have access to you when the baby comes, then there's nothing more you need to know."

She'd heard the Greek phrase "pillow friend" before. A woman with no claim to the man who provided for her until he tired of her and sent her away. Stephanie couldn't imagine anything so awful.

"It's either one or the other, Stephanie, because under no circumstances will I let you leave Greece now."

Nikos meant it with every breath of his body. As he'd told her earlier, this baby was doubly precious to him now.

How bizarre that she was hesitating, when she'd come to Greece to find her baby's father and do the right thing for her child. But nothing had gone the way she'd envisioned it. Theirs would be a marriage without love.

"When do you plan for us to be married?"

"Tomorrow."

So soon! "Isn't there a waiting period?"

"Not with my contacts."

Naturally, Nikos knew someone in high places who could move mountains. Of course he did! Stephanie didn't doubt he could make anything happen, if he wanted it enough. "Where will ours take place?"

"At the small church on Oinoussa, with Father Kerykes, the village priest. He performed Kon's marriage. The man can keep a confidence and be trusted to honor my wishes."

Stephanie moistened her lips nervously. At least they would exchange vows in a holy place.

"What's it going to be, Stephanie?"

As a marriage proposal, it lacked all the passion and romance of her dreams. Without looking at him, she said, "For our child's sake, I want to marry you to give it your name."

"In that case, follow me. I have something to show you."

He left the lounge and walked across the corridor to the locked door, which he opened with a key. It was another bedroom, with two twin beds. "You're welcome to look in the closet."

What on earth?

Stephanie stepped past him and opened the double doors. On one side she discovered two military dress uniforms hanging, one was white, the other navy blue with gold buttons and braid. Next to them was a pair of crutches.

When she glanced on the other side, she was startled to discover half a dozen rifles and a special black scuba diving suit, along with a ton of very official looking gear that would be used by someone in the military.

She turned slowly and sought his gaze. "This equipment belongs to you. What does it mean? I thought you worked for your family's company."

"I did until I was twenty-two. By then Kon was divorced and we decided to join the Greek navy, much to my father's chagrin. We were in for ten years, but for the last five we've been Navy SEALs doing covert operations for our government."

That's why he was such an expert scuba diver.... All those years, Nikos had been fighting for his country. So far every minute she'd spent with him since she'd flown here provided one revelation after another.

"While I was on vacation with you, our unit got called up to do another highly classified mission. Since I can never use my own identity when I travel, and had to leave immediately, the note I left you was the best I could do."

The memory of that note flashed through her mind. *Unfortunately, I've had to leave the island because of an emergency at my work that couldn't be handled by anyone else.* Stephanie was so stunned, she sank down on one of the beds for support.

"Two days later the enemy ambushed our underwater demolition team. They bombed out of the water the fishing vessel we were using for surveillance. After it was detonated, I saw one of them swim away, before I could warn everyone. Kon died in the explosion. I was knocked unconscious and would have died if I hadn't been picked up and flown to the hospital."

"Nikos—"

"At first I was told the injury to my spine meant I'd be paralyzed from the waist down, but slowly feeling came back to my limbs."

"Thank heaven," she whispered in a trembling voice.

"The explosion should have taken me out, too!" His own voice shook with despair.

"But it didn't, and you have to believe there was a reason you survived."

His grim expression devastated her. "If you can make me believe that, then you're a saint."

Anger swept through her. "Kon didn't leave a child behind, but you did! Think about the fact that you're not paralyzed. Otherwise your child would grow up knowing you only in a wheelchair."

He bit out a Greek epithet before he murmured, "It turned out I'd been deeply bruised, but I could walk."

"You're one of the lucky vets, Nikos, and it's going to mean the world to your child that you continue to get better and stronger. Are you seeing a doctor regularly?"

"Yes," he whispered.

"What about exercise?"

"Among his many jobs, Yannis helps me do mine up on deck."

"I can help you with them, too."

"That won't be necessary, but since you're going to be my wife, I wanted you to know about my past. Now we don't ever have to speak of it again."

Nikos closed the closet doors and pulled her cell phone from his pocket. "Before we make any plans, you need to talk to your boss and tell him you can't work for him anymore." He handed it to her. "While you do that, I'll be in the galley. Come and find me after you've talked to him. If I'm not there, I'll be in the lounge."

With her heart thudding, she got to her feet. "Nikos?"

He paused in the doorway, darting her a piercing glance. "What is it?"

With that intimidating look, the question she would have asked him never made it past her lips. In fact, she already did have the answer to what would have happened to them if he hadn't had to leave the island to go on a covert operation.

Nothing would have been different. Like her father, when he'd left her mother, Nikos would have said goodbye to Stephanie, telling her the lie that he'd see her again, and that would have been the end of it.

Until his accident, Nikos's future had been tied up with another woman. As he'd told Stephanie a little while ago, Natasa wanted children....

CHAPTER FIVE

WHEN NIKOS BROUGHT the dishes from the lounge into the galley, he found Yannis enjoying breakfast. The balding seaman needed a lot of food to keep going. He looked up. "What are your plans for today, Nikos?"

"After you finish eating, we'll pull up anchor and head for Oinoussas . Once we've docked I won't need you until tomorrow. That ought to give you some time to do what you want with Maria." The widow who ran a small shop had become his love interest.

"She'll like that."

"But not you?" he teased.

Yannis stared at him. "What's going on? You no longer act like you're on the way to your own funeral."

"I'm getting married tomorrow to Kyria Walsh at the church of Agios Dionysios. *That's* what's going on. I need to make preparations."

His longtime widower friend looked shocked. "Married? To her? But what about Kyria Lander?"

Nikos started doing the dishes. He and Yannis took turns cooking and cleaning up. "She's not pregnant with my child, Yannis. Stephanie is."

"Ah…" The older man crossed himself. "This happened while you were on vacation in the Caribbean?"

"Yes."

A huge smile broke out on his weathered face. "Now I understand. I told you the scuba diving there was the finest in the world. I'm glad you listened to me. She's a real beauty, Nikos. It's about time you had some happiness in your life. Does your father know?"

"Not yet." Nikos was functioning on faith that she was pregnant and carrying his baby.

"There will be an explosion when your family finds out."

"It won't matter, because by the time they hear the news, she'll be my wife. You're going to be a witness, like you were for Kon."

"I'll be honored. Are you having a boy?"

"It's too soon to know. Maybe in another month. For the present we'll live on the yacht. Stephanie needs pampering and must eat for two. Since the last time I saw her, she's lost her glow, and needs to take care of herself." He refused to entertain the thought that she wasn't pregnant.

The older man nodded.

"Just so you know, I've told her how I got injured." He turned his head away from Yannis. "We have no secrets."

His friend got up and added his plate and mug to the dishwasher. "That's good. Otherwise, she'll find out soon enough," he said before leaving the galley. Since Nikos knew that, he would take steps to make certain Stephanie remained clueless about his PTSD.

After reaching for another roll, he headed for the lounge to phone Father Kerykes. They talked for a few minutes to settle on a time for the wedding, which was finally arranged to take place at four in the afternoon.

Next Nikos called Tassos, who seemed overjoyed to learn about the imminent marriage. He insisted that his wife and the Gregerov family would all be there to join in the festivities and take pictures. Later they would treat the bridal couple to dinner at their favorite local taverna.

Just as Nikos hung up, Stephanie walked into the lounge. Her closed expression told him little. "Did you reach your boss?"

She nodded.

"How did he take the news?"

"He wasn't happy about it and complained it would be hard to find someone to replace me."

"I don't doubt it. You're an expert diver and swimmer."

"There are enough qualified applicants in the file drawer that he'll have no problem. It's my reason for resigning he doesn't like."

"How so?"

"Grant is the fatherly type and feels I haven't known you long enough to consider getting married."

"Did you tell him you're pregnant?"

"I had to, otherwise he wouldn't let it go. In the end he grudgingly wished me well and told me he was glad I wasn't going to make another flight back to Florida, considering my condition. He's really a wonderful man. I promised him that after the baby was born, I'd send him a picture of the three of us."

Nikos liked the sound of that. But what if none of it turned out to be true? He rubbed the back of his neck. *You can't afford to think like that, Vassalos.*

"He'll send me my final paycheck when I give him an address."

"Good. What about your friends?"

She lowered her head. "I'll phone them after we're married." She'd called Melinda from Chios to let her know she'd arrived safely. "Otherwise they'll tell me to wait. I can't deal with that kind of pressure right now."

Nikos knew all too well about pressure, especially the parental kind. "In that case let's go up on deck, where you can sunbathe on one of the loungers until we dock at Oinoussa. After that we'll enjoy lunch in town. Among other things we'll do some shopping for clothes, since you only packed enough for a day or two."

Her jewel-like blue eyes fastened on him in apprehension. "What other things?"

"When did your doctor want to see you again?"

"In a month."

"Was everything fine?"

"Yes, except that I need to take iron."

"I saw the pills. To be on the safe side I want to stop in at the clinic, so we can meet the doctor who'll be taking care of you from here on out. Dr. Panos looks after Elianna and Ariadne, who both live on Oinoussa and have great faith in him. You'll need to set up your next appointment."

To his surprise she looked relieved. "I'm glad you thought of a good doctor for me. I really like my OB. He was my mother's doctor and has cared for me since my teens. It's hard to gain trust with someone else."

It was hard to gain trust, period, but since she hadn't fought him on this, Nikos was in a better mood than he'd been since leaving the hospital more dead than alive.

They were coming in to dock at Oinoussa. To Stephanie it looked surprisingly large and beautiful. Tranquil.

The town appeared to be draped over green hillsides, with several churches and charming houses displaying more of the local neoclassical style. Nikos told her there were no springs, so the water came from wells and a reservoir.

She looked over the yacht railing to the brilliant blue water beneath them. Everything was so clean and calm, it almost didn't seem real. This heavenly island was going to be her new home. While Nikos talked of the many beaches she could explore, her mind was on her baby who would be born here, a baby whose father wasn't a New Yorker named Dev Harris.

It started to hit her that she'd done something miraculous for her child, something her own mother couldn't bring herself to do for Stephanie. Because she'd found Nikos, this baby would have a full identity from the very moment of its birth.

Experiencing a sensation of euphoria, she turned to Nikos, who'd come to stand next to her. His hard jawline and arresting Greek profile stood out against the white houses and tiled roofs in the distance.

Suddenly, his black-fringed eyes fused with hers. For a moment, the dullness that had robbed them of their vitality since she'd come here vanished, and they shone with that same energy she'd glimpsed on vacation. "What were you going to ask me?" he murmured in a voice an octave lower than normal.

Her heart raced, because there were times when they seemed to be so in sync, they could read each other's minds. "What's your full name?"

She watched his chest slowly rise and fall. "Theodoros Nikolaos Vassalos."

Stephanie blinked. "Is Theodoros your nickname?"

"No. I don't have a nickname. It's my father's name."

"So when our baby is born, it will take your name first?"

"Yes, because it will be our first and only child."

"Are there rules about naming it?"

"You can name our baby whatever you like."

"But what if we follow the rules?"

"Then if it's a boy, we'd name it Alexandros, after my father's father."

She experimented outloud. "Nikolaos Alexandros Vassalos."

"That's right."

"And if it's a girl?"

"After my mother's mother, Melitta."

"I like both names. Are they still alive?"

"Yes."

She smiled up at him. "Our child will have great-grandparents, too. What a blessing," she said as he studied her hair and features.

"Nikos?" Yannis called out.

"I'm coming," he said, still staring at her with an enigmatic expression she couldn't read. "Get what you need to take with you. We're going ashore."

On legs that felt like mush, she hurried downstairs to freshen up and gather her purse. In a few minutes the men had secured the ropes, and Nikos walked her along the dock to a parking area, where he helped her into a dark blue car.

"Feel free to use this whenever you want to come into town. I'll give you a key when we're back on the yacht."

"Thank you."

She noticed he moved a little slower, but consid-

ering his horrendous accident, it was miraculous he
could walk without most people noticing anything was
wrong.

"Are you hungry?" he asked.

"I'm getting there."

"Did you take your pill for nausea?"

"Just a few minutes ago."

"Good. There's a taverna where you eat in the garden at the back. I'll introduce you to some authentic
food I love."

Stephanie couldn't wait to see what he chose for
them, especially since these islands were home to him
and he knew the streets and shops like the back of his
hand.

The proprietor of the small restaurant beamed when
Nikos escorted her inside. They spoke in rapid Greek
before the older man led them through some doors to
a charming garden in bloom with fabulous wild hya-
cinths and orchids.

There were a dozen or so tables filled with tourists and locals. After settling at a table for two, they
were brought fruit drinks and appetizers. One dish,
something yellow, was prepared with olive oil, onions
and fava beans, Nikos told her. Another, called *caciki*,
tasted like cream cheese with cucumber and was served
with slices of freshly baked, crusty *psomi* bread. It was
followed by shrimp risotto and the grilled calamari.

Stephanie made inroads on everything but the oc-
topus. "Maybe another time," she said to him. After
his morose, brooding demeanor yesterday, the white
smile he suddenly flashed her, the first she'd seen since
her arrival, was so unexpected and startling that her

breath caught. She found herself praying this side of him wouldn't disappear.

"Dessert?"

He had to be teasing her. She shook her head. "Thank you. The meal was delicious, but I couldn't possibly eat another bite or it might turn on me."

"Since we can't have that, let's go buy you some clothes."

They went back to the car and he drove to the other side of the village, where he stopped in front of a boutique. "Ariadne likes this store. She says it's trendy. I think you'll find something to your taste."

Inside, Stephanie discovered some great short-sleeved tops, pants, skirts, a couple sundresses and several dressy, long-sleeved blouses in filmy material for evening. Along with those she bought more lingerie, sleepwear and a bikini.

An older woman waiting on her spoke excellent English and was very helpful. As she was putting a white sundress and jacket with small purple violets around the hem in a box for Stephanie, she said, "You will look beautiful in this."

"Thank you."

Nikos stood at the counter with her. "It will make a lovely wedding dress, don't you think?"

Stephanie's heart plummeted. She knew Nikos wanted their wedding to be simple, but she'd still hoped to wear something more bridal to her own nuptials. The saleswoman must have seen her reaction, because to Stephanie's surprise she frowned at Nikos.

"A wedding dress? Oh, no. For that you need to go across the street."

"It's all right," she quickly told the woman.

In order not to upset Nikos, Stephanie forced herself to recover from her disappointment in a big hurry. "I love this dress. It will be perfect. Here's my credit card." She'd come to Greece unprepared, and didn't expect him to pay for a new wardrobe.

Too late, she realized her mistake. In front of the other woman he took the card away and replaced it with one from his wallet. Stephanie gave him a covert glance and saw that his dark expression was back. She should have guessed Nikos had too much pride to allow a woman to pay.

There were so many things she needed to learn about him. On the island they hadn't gone anywhere except the resort, rarely interacting with anyone other than the staff. This was a totally different situation.

He collected her purchases and walked her out to the car, putting everything in the backseat. While he did that, she climbed in the front passenger seat, but he held on to her door so she couldn't close it.

Stephanie looked up at him. "Aren't we going to leave?"

His jaw had hardened. "I saw the look on your face in there. You want a traditional wedding dress? We'll get you one. The most elaborate we can find."

She was crushed. "No, Nikos. Please get in the car so we can talk without everyone hearing us."

"There's nothing to discuss. Come."

After she got out, because he'd left her no choice, he locked the car and ushered her across the street to the bridal shop. An elegant, striking young woman, probably in her mid-twenties, caught sight of Nikos and couldn't look anywhere else. When she spoke in Greek, he responded in English.

"We'd like to see your designer bridal gowns for my fiancée."

Fiancée. What a joke.

"Right over here." She led them to a rack of sumptuous-looking dresses with price tags that meant this was a high end shop. "Go ahead and start looking."

Stephanie hated being in this position. The whole time she examined each dress, she could hear the ringless clerk talking to Nikos in Greek instead of waiting on her. The younger woman was deliberately flirting with him. Stephanie had to get a grip. In the mood he was in, she knew he wouldn't leave this shop until she'd found something for their wedding.

Last night, when she'd opened the closet containing his uniforms, she'd imagined him as a groom wearing the navy one with the gold buttons. With his black hair and olive skin, he'd look magnificent in it. Such an outfit required a wedding dress that lived up to it. If he was now intent on her wearing a designer gown, then she expected him to dress accordingly, too.

After some deliberation, she chose the most expensive dress on the rack. It was a simple princess style, but the floor-length veil of Alençon lace gave it elegance. It cost a fortune, but she didn't care. He'd accused her of using him for his money. *So be it.*

She turned to the clerk. "If you have this one in stock, I'll take it. In America I'm a size 4." Of course, Stephanie wouldn't be that size much longer, but she figured she could squeeze into it once she'd worn off her meal.

The clerk looked taken back. "I believe we do."

"Then please ring it up for me. My *fiancé* will carry it out to our car. Thank you."

Once the clerk went into the back room, Stephanie glanced at Nikos, who was leaning against the counter, his face implacable. No doubt he was feeling some pain, but he'd hate it if she drew attention to it. Maybe she could give him an out.

"Do you still want to stop by the clinic before we go back to the yacht? We could go there tomorrow instead."

His black eyes had taken on that glittery cast. "There's still time this afternoon, unless you're not feeling well."

She wasn't. Not exactly. But for once it had nothing to do with nausea. She sensed he still didn't trust her, and could cry her eyes out after the lovely meal at the restaurant, where he'd been more like…like Dev. "I'm fine."

Stephanie turned her back while he dealt with the saleswoman, then they left the shop.

He laid the dress and veil on top of the other packages before they left for the clinic, which appeared to be closer to the port.

When they went inside to Reception, they learned that Dr. Panos was operating and wouldn't be available. Not to be thwarted, Nikos made an appointment for her for September 1, a full workup.

With that accomplished, they drove to the parking area at the dock. He let her take a few bags, but he carried the rest, along with her wedding finery. Nikos should have brought his cane and let her do more to help, but that infernal pride of his got in the way.

Odd how she hadn't seen it manifest itself when they'd been on vacation. He'd been so mellow and easy-going then. She longed for that time to come back, but it never would.

Once he'd carried everything to her bedroom, he told her he'd be on the phone in the lounge if she needed him. For the next little while Stephanie removed the tags from her purchases and put them away in the closet and dresser.

She checked her watch. It was going on five o'clock. By this time tomorrow they would have been married an hour already.

She supposed she should try on her wedding dress, but for the moment she was too tired, and she'd need a shower first. Emotional fatigue had set in. Maybe later, after she got ready for bed, she'd take it out of the plastic cover and see how it looked on her.

With a sigh she removed her jeans, which were too tight, and lay down on the bed for a minute. She turned on her side, while her hand went automatically to the little bulge, which was definitely getting bigger. Tears trickled out of the corners of her eyes.

"All this is for you, my darling. Are you a little Alex who will be impossibly handsome like your father and turn the head of every girl? Or are you a beautiful little Melitta with flashing black eyes and hair like your daddy? Maybe by my next appointment, or the next, I'll know what to call you."

CHAPTER SIX

WHEN IT GOT to be seven, Nikos hung up the phone with the florist who would bring some flowers to the church tomorrow. All he had left to do was buy a ring. He'd do it in the morning, after Yannis came on board and Nikos had done his exercises.

Now that he'd taken care of everything he could, he got up and walked down the corridor to Stephanie's bedroom. He knocked, but couldn't hear any noise. Since he would have noticed if she'd gone up on deck, he knocked again.

Was she sick? She'd eaten more at lunch than he'd expected. Though he was relieved to see she had an appetite, he worried. Being very quiet, he turned the handle and opened the door a crack.

What he saw made his heart fail. Stephanie had removed her jeans and left them on the floor where she'd stepped out of them. Could he hope it was because they were too tight?

She was out for the count, with her long gorgeous legs uncovered. Jet lag had caught up to her. Her gilt-blond hair splayed out on the pillow. He'd seen this sight before, when she hadn't been wearing any clothes.

The memories came rushing back, increasing the

ache for her that had never gone away. Before he lost control, he closed the door and went to the galley to fix himself a cup of coffee and throw a salad together. Anything to keep busy. When she awakened, he assumed she'd want some dinner.

Nikos had just added the feta cheese when she appeared in the doorway. He shot her a glance. She was wearing a new pair of jeans and one of the flowered print blouses she'd picked out, this one in aqua and white. He noticed that she'd brushed her hair. Beneath the light it shone a silvery-gold, and given those dazzling blue eyes of hers, he'd never seen a woman with such fabulous coloring.

"At last."

"I didn't mean to sleep so long."

"You're still catching up. Are you hungry?"

"I am, if you can believe it. I just took another pill to make sure I stay feeling good."

"It seems to be working. Come all the way in and join me."

He'd already set the galley table with fresh fruit and rolls, plus apple juice and water for her. After serving the salad, he poured himself coffee and sat down opposite her. She reached for the water first and drank a full glass before eating a roll.

"The hot weather this time of year will get to you if you don't stay hydrated."

"So I've noticed. I'll start carrying a bottle around with me. Thank you for fixing dinner, but I hope you know I don't expect to be waited on."

"I enjoyed fixing our prenuptial meal."

She ate some of her salad, then rested her fork on the plate. "Speaking of our wedding, I'd like to explain about today. I didn't want to leave the impression that the white sundress wasn't good enough to wear at the church."

"You owe me no explanation."

"Yes, I do." She wiped the corner of her mouth with a napkin. "The clerk at the boutique mirrored my surprise, but she shouldn't have said anything."

"It's fortunate she did. As I understand it, the wedding day is for the bride."

Defeated by his attitude, she said, "You're right. Women are hopeless romantics in that department, but for me it's more than that. I know you wanted to keep the marriage simple, and I would have been perfectly happy with that if I wasn't pregnant, and our situation was different."

"What do you mean, different?" His question came out sounding like ripping silk, alarming her.

"We're not marrying for the normal reason and I've been thinking about the baby. When it's old enough, our child will want to see pictures of the wedding. Blame it on me for wanting to give it everything I was denied.

"I'm sure there are wedding pictures at your parents' home, of them in their finery. A child wants to see what its mother and father looked like on that special day, the way they wore their hair, what they were wearing. The moment I opened the closet in the extra bedroom, I could envision you in the navy blue uniform."

She leaned toward him excitedly. "Think what it would mean to our child to see you in it on your wedding day. He or she will know about your injury and why you had to leave the service earlier than you'd planned. It'll be preserving a piece of history.

"I have no history from my father, but you can leave some for our child. That's why I chose the dress in the bridal shop with the long lace veil. I know it was expensive, but the sundress wouldn't do justice to your uniform. There's nothing like a handsome man in his dress blues. Any woman would tell you the same thing."

"Stephanie—"

She took a quick breath. "Don't deny it. You *are* exceptional, Nikos. My friends on the island never did get over you. The girl in the bridal shop couldn't take her eyes off you, either. Our son or daughter will be so proud of you and the honorable way you served your country."

Nikos jumped up from the table, too full of conflicting emotions to sit there any longer. He'd leaped to the wrong conclusion after she'd chosen the most expensive gown in the shop. How easily his trust had worn thin. But he'd been remembering the conversation with his father.

You've never looked at Natasa or any woman the way you're looking at this female viper. I admit she's devilishly ravishing in that American way, but she's a mercenary viper nonetheless, one who knows your monetary worth and has come to trap you.

"Don't make me out to be a hero, Stephanie."

"Any man or woman who serves in the military is a hero, Nikos. I'll make two albums to preserve our wedding day. One for our child and one for your parents. Maybe Yannis will take pictures for us." After a pause, she added, "And perhaps the day will come when you'll tell me what they did to you that was so terrible you don't want them at the wedding."

Without looking at her he said, "My reasons run

fathoms deep, but they have nothing to do with you."
He doubted he could ever talk about it.

"Still, they *are* your parents and our baby's grandparents. I know an album of our wedding day will
mean everything to them, too. Please tell me you'll
wear the uniform."

"I'll think about it," he muttered. "I have to go
ashore again. When I leave, I'll set the security system. If it goes off, the harbor police will be alerted and
a signal will be sent to my cell phone. You'll be perfectly safe while I'm gone."

"Where are you going?"

"If you must know, to visit a friend."

"Tassos? Have you told him about the baby?"

"No one knows except Yannis. I'll see you in the
morning."

He left the boat and took off for the cemetery. It
would be his first visit to Kon's grave. Nikos had been
in the hospital when his buddy had been buried in the
Gregerov family plot. They'd always talked over everything important....

At three-thirty the next afternoon, Nikos waited at the
car, ready to take pictures that he knew were so essen-
tial to Stephanie's happiness. After breakfast he'd gone
into town to purchase her ring. When he returned, he'd
discussed the details of the wedding ritual with her.
Now it was time to go.

In a moment she stepped off the yacht. With Yannis's help she started walking along the dock in her
wedding dress. He doubted there'd ever been a sight
like her before, and he started clicking frame after
frame.

The few people around the port watching her would think they were seeing a heavenly vision of femininity in flowing white silk. Angel hair glinted silver and gold through the lace in the late afternoon sun. His throat swelled with emotion to realize this bride was going to be his.

In his gut he wanted the child she was carrying to be his. If it wasn't...

After seeing those jeans lying on the floor at the side of her bed last evening, he was convinced she was pregnant. He couldn't let any more doubts ruin today, which would never come again.

Stephanie's urgent plea had gotten to him and he'd put on his dress blue uniform. With nothing more than a few clues, she'd come all the way from Florida to find him, so he would know he was going to be a father. The least he could do was accede to her desires on this issue. He'd told Kon as much.

Nikos had been thinking a lot about Stephanie's father. Maybe he could be found through the help of a good private investigator. It was worth looking into, but that would have to wait until another day.

Yannis, acting in the place of her father, who would probably have given her away if he'd known of her existence, had worn his best white suit for the occasion. Nikos suspected the older seaman was enjoying this. He and Stephanie seemed to be getting along well already. Yannis was an old softie beneath his gruff looking exterior. It was clear she had already charmed him.

Nikos kept taking pictures until they reached the car. Her eyes, so solemn, met his for an instant before Yannis took over, asking them to pose together before they got inside. After some careful maneuvering to protect her dress, they helped her into the backseat, and Nikos sat in front while Yannis drove.

"Oh, Nikos!" she cried softly when they'd traveled a distance up the hillside. The small domed gray-and-white church of Agios Dionysios stood overlooking the sea. "How beautiful! I can't believe we're going to be married here."

"My wife and I were married in that same church forty years ago," Yannis said over his shoulder.

"Were you childhood sweethearts?"

"How did you know?"

Her gentle chuckle found new areas inside Nikos's body to warm. "Do you have children?"

"Two married sons and six grandchildren. They're fishermen and live here."

"You're a very lucky man."

"It was a lucky day when Nikos met you."

Well, well. Stephanie's takeover of Yannis was now complete.

"Thank you, Yannis."

The next few minutes were a blur as they pulled up to the church's parking area, where the Gregerov family was waiting *en masse* to greet them. Nikos introduced her to Tassos's parents, Castor and Tiana Gregerov, and his pretty wife, Elianna, who had dark blond hair. The other women were various shades of brunette. More pictures were taken. Nikos had hired a professional photographer to film everything.

In the rush he noticed Tassos reach for Stephanie and press something in her hand. Nikos was curious to know what it was, but he would have to wait. He saw her eyes glisten with tears before she kissed him on the cheek.

After embracing Tassos's mother, Nikos reached for Stephanie and they proceeded inside the church. He cupped her elbow, taking care with her veil, and walked to the front, where a dozen sprays of flowers filled the nave with perfume. He'd made certain there were some gardenias among the arrangements.

He had the distinct impression Stephanie was pacing herself carefully in deference to him not being able to move quite so fast. Small courtesies seemed to come naturally to her, another trait he couldn't help but admire.

Father Kerykes chatted with them before asking Tassos and Yannis to take their places on either side of the couple. The others sat in a group. For Stephanie's sake he presided in English, promising to keep it as short as possible. But as Nikos had explained to Stephanie earlier, there was no such thing as a short Greek wedding.

First came the service of the betrothal with the rings. Nikos had bought her a diamond ring, and a gold band for her to give to him, but she produced a ring he immediately recognized as Kon's. Nikos was so moved by Tassos's gesture, he choked up during the marriage sacrament.

It was followed by the crowning and ceremonial walk. Three times around the priest, who at the end removed their flowers. After they kissed the Bible, he pronounced his blessing on them.

"For better or worse, you're Mrs. Vassalos now," Nikos whispered as they walked down the aisle holding hands. "Are you feeling all right?"

"I—I'm fine." Her voice faltered. "Just thirsty."

"There's water in the vestibule, where we'll sign the documents. Then we'll go outside for more pictures."

By the time she emerged from the church with her bouquet, her cheeks looked flushed. Nikos urged everyone to hurry with the well-wishing and the pictures, but all of them were pressing for the bridal kiss. He did it swiftly, noticing Stephanie was fading fast. No wonder there was little response.

"Are you going to be sick?" he asked as he helped her into the car.

"No," she replied, but her voice trembled. "I'm just feeling weak and overheated. I'll be all right in a minute."

"In this weather a wedding like ours is brutal, but it's over now. The taverna will be cool. It's only a mile away. Drive fast, Yannis."

"I feel a fraud, Nikos. I'm a hot weather girl and don't know what happened to me in there."

"You're pregnant and have been through an arduous marriage ritual."

She lay back in the corner with her eyes closed. "Once was enough. I fought so hard not to faint in front of you."

"You made it. I'm very proud of you."

Stephanie started laughing. "I had no idea it would be an endurance test."

"Why do you think I put it off all these years?" he teased.

"Sorry. You must be stifling in your uniform. In hindsight I can see why you wanted me to wear the sundress." She let out a little moan. "I shouldn't have tried to find you in the first place. It forced you to have to go through all this."

With those words he felt as if he'd been rammed in the chest. She had no idea what was going through his mind. *"Don't ever say that again."*

Stephanie groaned. She'd said the wrong thing and had upset him, but it was the truth.

She might not have forced him with a sniper's rifle, like the ones in his closet. But the chance that this baby *could* be his had served as the ultimate weapon. Stephanie wasn't a fool. She knew he had doubts about its true paternity and wouldn't be satisfied until a DNA test was done, thus the reason for bringing up the possibility of divorce.

Over the last three months her heart had been hardened against him for his desertion of her, only to be softened after he'd insisted on either keeping her as his mistress or marrying her for the sake of their unborn child.

The *only* child he would ever have...

Their child, who would know its father and love him.

That's what this whole day had been about. She couldn't lose sight of that pertinent reality. After letting out an anxious sigh, she sat up straighter in the seat. "Forgive me for my show of temper. I can be a crosspatch sometimes. This has been a beautiful day and a wedding every bride dreams of. The flowers were beautiful and I love my ring. Thank you for making it all possible, Nikos."

"As long as you're feeling better and there's no harm to the baby, it's all that matters."

His need to protect had come out. No wonder he'd

snapped. She had to remember that and watch what she said from now on.

"We're headed for the most traditional taverna on the island, where there are few tourists. The owner's family makes their pasta and *dolmadakia* by hand. Besides oven-baked lamb and spit roast with lemon potatoes and garlic, you'll enjoy stuffed zucchini and meatballs, called *keftedes,* that melt in your mouth."

"I love meatballs."

"They're made in a tomato sauce that's out of this world."

Nikos sounded hungry.

Within fifteen minutes they were all assembled inside the authentic Greek restaurant, where everyone laughed and ate with great relish to the accompaniment of music. Stephanie found Kon's family members charming and felt the women's acceptance.

More pictures were taken, and toasts rendered, along with speeches from everyone including Yannis. It was clear they all loved Nikos. At one point he reached for her and kissed her warmly several times on the mouth, to the delight of their wedding party.

She couldn't drink alcohol and instead opted for a spoon sweet, which was a fruit embedded in syrup. "You taste delicious," he murmured as she kissed him back, always telling herself it was for the pictures that would go in the family album.

The evening wore on in a celebration she would always cherish, but when she looked around, she felt an ache in her heart that Nikos's family wasn't a part of it. As for herself, she wished her mother were still alive and could have been here.

If there'd been time, Stephanie would have invited

her friends who'd met Nikos on vacation. But it wasn't meant to be, because this had been pulled together on an emergency basis. Every flash of light from the diamond solitaire on her finger seemed to be sending a warning. *You may have had a wedding with all the trappings, but remember, it's the baby he wants, if it's his....*

She felt Nikos's gaze on her. "It's still too warm in here for you. I can see your eyelids are drooping. It's time to get you back home to bed, where you'll be cooler."

He stood up and announced they were leaving. "Stephanie and I thank you for making this day the most memorable of our lives." On that note he ushered her out of the taverna. Twilight had stolen over the island, giving it a magical feel. Nikos helped her into the car. Once more Yannis drove them down the hillside.

In the distance she saw the yacht. Nikos had called it home. Until he bought them a place here on the island to live, it would be hers, too.

Tassos and Elianna had followed them and brought half a dozen of the flower sprays from the church to decorate the lower lounge. His kindness today had touched her deeply and she gave him a hug before Nikos went up on deck with him. Besides being a good friend, he and her brand-new husband were in business together and had a lot to talk about.

Elianna started to leave, but Stephanie touched her arm. "Before you go, would you mind unbuttoning the back of my dress?" She put her veil on the couch to make it easier.

An odd smile broke out on the other woman's face. "You don't want Nikos to do it?"

Stephanie averted her eyes. "He wants to talk to Tassos right now."

"If you're sure."

"I am."

Elianna got busy. "It's the most beautiful dress I ever saw. How did you get it fastened?"

"Yannis helped me."

She let out a quiet laugh. "With all these buttons, it must have taken quite a while. Nikos didn't mind?"

"Yannis told Nikos to go away so he wouldn't see me until we left for the church."

"You are the envy of every woman in the Oinousses. People here thought he would marry Natasa Lander."

"I understand she's very lovely."

"Yes, and very rich. Her family is in shipping, too. They have the largest mansion on Chios Island. Nikos has surprised everyone."

"Our marriage surprised me, too," Stephanie said in a tremulous voice.

"Tassos tells me you two met on vacation in the Caribbean before the explosion happened."

"Yes. We were both scuba diving and paired up to explore." She was tempted to tell Elianna she was pregnant, but then thought the better of it, since Nikos hadn't chosen to tell Tassos yet.

"Ah. Nikos and Kon tried to teach me, but I got too frightened and couldn't control my breathing. I panicked."

"With more practice, you can overcome your fear of it, Elianna. I'd be happy to work with you if you'd like."

"Tassos wants me to dive with him."

"It's a beautiful world under the sea. If you can shake your fear, you'll learn to love it."

Stephanie felt the last button release and turned around. "What do you say?"

"Maybe I'll try again with your help."

"That's wonderful! I'll call you in a few days. We'll have lunch and make plans. Bring your baby. How old is he?"

"Theo is ten months and trying to walk."

"I can't wait to see him."

Elianna's dark brown eyes widened in surprise. "You won't be on your honeymoon?"

"We already had ours in the Caribbean. Right now Nikos is anxious to get started on the drilling with your husband. Since the accident that killed Kon, Yannis tells me he's been morose and unhappy. Now that he can't be in the navy, he needs to plunge into something else."

The other woman nodded. "Everyone took Kon's death hard, especially Tassos. He's thrilled that Nikos is interested in his ideas to start their own company."

"Then we need to help them. Right?"

They stared at each other for a moment before she nodded. "Yes. I'm glad he married you."

"I'm glad, too." If Elianna only knew the half of it. "Thank you for helping me." She gave her a hug before they parted.

While Tassos's wife disappeared up the stairs, Stephanie reached for the veil and walked down the hall to her bedroom to remove her wedding finery. First she stepped out of her dress and underskirt, which she hung in the closet. What a relief, so her stomach could expand! Another week and she wouldn't have been able to wear a size 4. The shop probably wouldn't have sold that gown any larger.

After a quick shower, she wrapped herself in her plaid flannel robe, then folded the veil with care and put it on the shelf above. Since she had no idea how long Nikos would be, she decided now would be the perfect time to phone Melinda.

With the room pleasantly cool, she lay down on top of the bed to make the call. So much had happened since her arrival in Greece, it felt like a century instead of a few days since she'd talked to her friend, let alone seen her.

After three rings Melinda picked up. "I'm so glad it's you, Steph. I've been worried."

"Don't be. Everything's fine. I have a lot to tell you, but if this is a bad time—"

"No, no. I'm taking a late lunch. Tell me what's going on. I'm dying to know how your hunch is panning out. Are you onto anything?"

Stephanie sat up, almost crushing the phone in her hand. "I found him, Melinda."

"You're kidding…"

"No. His real name is Nikos Vassalos. I don't know how much time I have before he comes to find me, so I'll make this quick."

For the next few minutes she told her what she could, ending with, "We were married a little while ago and now we're back on the yacht."

"Wait, wait, wait. You're *married?*"

"Yes, and I won't be coming back to Florida until after the baby is born and it's safe to fly." A noise in the hall attracted her attention, followed by a tap on the door. "Listen, Melinda— I'm not alone. I'll have to call you tomorrow. *Ciao.*"

She hung up and tightened the belt on her robe before opening the door. Nikos was still dressed in his uniform. His dark gorgeous looks affected her the same way they'd done on the island when she'd first laid eyes on him. She couldn't breathe then, either.

"I take it Tassos and Elianna have gone?"

He nodded. "I could hear your voice just now."

"Yes. I was talking to Melinda."

His black eyes searched the depths of hers. "Elianna told me you've invited her over in a few days."

Nervous, Stephanie clasped the lapels of her robe. "Yes, if that's all right. But if you have other plans for us, I'll phone her and we'll decide on a later time for a visit. I just assumed you would want to get back to work." When he didn't respond, she added, "Ours isn't a conventional marriage, and my coming to Greece interrupted everything. I don't want you to think you have to entertain me."

"Elianna told me you were going to try and help her get over her fear of scuba diving. How did she know you're an expert?"

At the way his brows furrowed, alarm shot through Stephanie's body. "While she was helping me out of my dress, I mentioned that we met scuba diving in the Caribbean. Did I say something wrong?"

He undid his tie and removed it in a way that made her pulse pick up speed. "Have you forgotten you're having a baby? You told me you were giving up diving."

"Nikos…that doesn't mean I can't swim at all. A little exercise for pleasure will be good for me. As for helping her, I won't be descending with her. I'll only work with her on the surface and encourage her until she overcomes her fear. Tassos wants her to do it, but she would probably feel better around someone like me who doesn't intimidate her."

"You mean Tassos *does,*" Nikos drawled in a tone with an edge.

"He's her husband. She wants him to be proud of her, not watch her struggle."

In a quick move Nikos unbuttoned the jacket of his uniform. "Anytime you go in the water, I intend to be close by." With that parting remark, he started walking down the corridor.

"Wait..."

He paused midstride and looked back.

"Is Yannis still on board?"

"No. He won't be coming until morning. Why?"

That meant they weren't going out to sea. "I just wanted to thank him for everything he did for me today."

Nikos turned to face her. "It was no penance for him to button you up. He asked my permission, by the way. Yannis was worried you had no one to attend you."

Silly as it was, she felt heat swarm her cheeks. "He was very sweet."

"You can tell him that tomorrow."

She shoved her hands in her robe pockets. "Let me thank you now for making this day perfect. The Gregerov family couldn't have been kinder. I can see why you feel so close to them. I—I wish I'd been able to meet Kon." She stuttered over the words. "Your heart must have been touched to receive his ring."

"You can't imagine. It belonged to his grandfather, who gave it to him before he died. Kon wore it until he entered the military, then put it away to make sure nothing would happen to it until he retired. He planned to give it to a son if he ever had one."

Stephanie heard tears in Nikos's voice. She wasn't at all surprised at the depth of his grief and understood more than ever why she'd found him so broken when she'd first collided with him on board. "I'm sure Kon would have wanted you to have it."

She bit her lip, not knowing what else to say to comfort him. In fact, she feared her talking was irritating him. "Do you mind if I go up on deck for a while?"

He gave an elegant shrug of his shoulders. "This is your home. You can do whatever you like. When I was in town this morning, I bought some English speaking films on disk, which you can watch in the lounge. I won't set the security alarm until we're ready for bed."

"Thank you," she said to his retreating back.

After drinking some water from the galley, Stephanie went up on deck to take in the wonder of the night. She'd always lived by the water, but no place in her experience lived up to the beauty of these isolated islands set like glittering jewels on dark velvet.

Time passed, but Nikos still didn't join her. She had assumed that, in marrying her, he intended to sleep with her. She didn't know and he hadn't spelled out a detail like that, but without love on his part, she wouldn't be able to respond.

The problem was this was their wedding night. The kisses he'd given her at the restaurant had felt like a prelude to making love, but maybe they'd been for show. *For the photographs.*

Deciding not to wait for him any longer, she went below. There was no sign of him in the lounge. She could go down the hall and knock on his door. Was he waiting for her to come to him? Stephanie had no idea what to do. When they'd been together on the island, he'd never left her alone.

But they weren't married then, and he'd never intended to propose to her. They'd found intense pleasure together, but in his mind it had been temporary until he returned to his unit and ultimately to Natasa Lander.

Even leaving the other woman out of it, the more Stephanie thought about the situation, the more she understood that if he still didn't believe she was carrying his child, he wouldn't want to sleep with her. Maybe the thought was distasteful, even repugnant to him. Shivering at the possibility, she made up her mind never to expect a physical relationship with him.

After brushing her teeth, she took a pill and turned out the light. But once she was under the covers another thought came to her, with such force she let out a small cry and sat up. She didn't know why she hadn't considered it before. Since he was sterile, it was more than possible he was impotent, too.

Nikos...

If that was the case, then her heart grieved for him. He was such a proud man, it was only natural that since the explosion he wouldn't want to marry Natasa or *any* woman.

But he'd trusted Stephanie enough to marry her in order to give their child a father. In the process he'd become her husband in name only, to make it legitimate while he waited to find out the results of the DNA test. The dots were lining up.

No wonder he hadn't wanted his family to be a part

of today's nuptials. Everything was based on whether or not he was the father. She fell back and buried her face in the pillow to stifle her tears until oblivion took over.

CHAPTER SEVEN

THERE WAS AN animal suffering in the darkness. Stephanie kept looking for it, but couldn't find it. The whimpering turned into moans, torturing her. If only she could do something to help it. When it let out a piercing cry, the sound brought her awake.

All this time she'd been dreaming!

Trembling, she shot out of bed, incredulous that her mind had conjured anything so terrible. Something she'd eaten at the restaurant must not have agreed with her. Maybe a drink of water would help. She hurried to the bathroom. When she reached for a cup, her watch said 3:30.

After draining it, she went back to bed, but before she could fall asleep again she heard another blood-curdling cry. This time she wasn't dreaming. Without hesitation she threw on her robe and ran down the hall to Nikos's room. Though she knocked several times, he didn't respond. That was odd.

She knocked again before turning the door handle, hoping he wouldn't mind the intrusion. One glance inside the room told her he hadn't been to bed. It was still made. Had he gone to town?

Again she heard a moan, louder this time. It was

coming from the deck. An animal had to be trapped there. Maybe a cat or a dog, but she hadn't heard the security alarm go off. Needing something to protect her, she grabbed a fluffy bath towel from the bathroom and gingerly went up the stairs.

Once she was on deck the cry sounded like human sobbing. It was coming from the area of the transom. She walked toward it, then stopped dead in her tracks. There, crouching on the floor, was a man in a pair of sweats and nothing else. A crumpled blanket and sun bed lay nearby. He was on his knees with his head in his hands. As she got closer, she put a palm over her mouth.

Nikos!

Except it wasn't the man she knew. This version of him wasn't cognizant of the world right now. In a deep sleep, he was heaving great sobs, and fell over on his side. In the moonlight his tortured features glistened with moisture. Greek words broke from his lips. She couldn't make out anything except Kon's name, which he cried over and over again.

He'd been reliving the explosion. She knew about PTSD, but she'd never been with someone who was in the middle of a flashback. Without conscious thought she sank down on the sunbed next to him and put her arms around him.

"Nikos, wake up! This is just a bad dream." She rocked him for a few minutes, but he was too immersed. At one point he grasped her arm and let out a scream that raised the hairs on the back of her neck.

"It's all right, Nikos. It's over. Go back to sleep."

He twisted and turned, but held on while he sobbed on and off for another half hour. His fingers bit into her skin through the thin material of her robe, with such force she knew she'd have bruises. As terrifying as it was to see him like this, she felt a new closeness to him. His cries let her into his psyche, where he suffered. He'd seen the horrors of war, but the explosion that blew up his friend had traumatized him dramatically, and she was a vicarious witness.

Her gaze flew to Kon's ring. The reminder of their friendship must have set him off during his sleep. While she kissed Nikos's face, she put her leg over his to help quiet him, and murmured endearments.

Nothing seemed to help. Not at first. Then slowly, his fingers slid away and he fell quiet. Yannis would know all about this. Tomorrow Stephanie would get him alone and find out the name of Nikos's doctor. He needed help getting through his nightmares.

She held on to him. He'd said this yacht was home to him now. Had he decided to sleep up here? If so, how often did he do that? A few days ago, when she'd explored the lower deck, she'd noticed his unmade bed. The poor darling had probably suffered these incidents since being hospitalized.

Did he have more than one episode a night? She'd read that a flashback could be triggered by something and come on at any time. While he stayed on this yacht, he could be away from people.

It made perfect sense that he didn't want to be with family. But what if he hurt himself while up here on deck? What if he walked in his sleep and fell overboard? She'd heard the military wouldn't take sleepwalkers because they could be a danger to themselves and others.

After a few more minutes she eased away from him

and got to her feet. In his trauma, he'd flung his arm around and his elbow had caught the corner of her jaw. Both it and her arm felt sore, but it didn't matter. She covered him with the blanket, then reached for the towel and sat down in the lounger to watch over him. It was quarter to six. Who knew how long he'd sleep?

Since her arrival, he'd been watching her like a hawk because of the baby. What an irony, since it was *his* welfare she would be worrying about, along with her own, from here on out! He could injure himself without realizing it. She couldn't bear it if anything happened to him.

Before this new day was over, she planned to talk to his doctor. Nikos needed watching. One thing was certain: Stephanie wouldn't let him go to bed without her. Wherever he chose to sleep, that's where she'd be.

She'd sat there for another half hour when she saw Yannis come on board. The second their gazes met, she got up without making a sound and padded across the deck toward him.

"So you know," he whispered with a grave expression.

"Yes. I heard him during the night and came up to investigate. He's resting now, but I need to talk to his doctor."

He nodded. "The one he sees now is at the main clinic here on the island." The same place her new OB practiced. "His name is Dr. Ganis."

"Thank you. I'm glad you're back. I don't want him to know I heard anything until I've talked to the doctor."

"I think that would be best."

"Does he have flashbacks often?"

"Since he got out of the hospital, he had one the first night on the yacht, and last night."

"The wedding must have triggered thoughts of Kon. I'd better go below so he doesn't know I was up here."

"That's a good idea. He'll notice the red mark along your jaw."

Yannis didn't miss much. "I'll cover it with makeup." She patted his arm before hurrying toward the stairs.

The first thing she did on entering her room was get the card for her appointment out of her purse. Once she found it, she phoned the off-hours service at the clinic and left word for Dr. Ganis to call her back ASAP. As soon as she mentioned it was Mrs. Nikos Vassalos calling about her husband, the receptionist said she'd get in touch with the doctor right away.

For the next hour Stephanie got ready for the day. First her pills, then she took a shower and washed her hair. By the time she'd finished blow drying it, marks had come out on her left arm. She'd been afraid of that.

An application of makeup to the small blotch near her chin helped, plus a coating of mango frost lipstick. Then she headed for the closet. Stephanie thanked providence she'd had the foresight to buy a long-sleeved blouse. It was an all-over print in a gauzy fabric that hung just below the waist. She put it on and matched it with a pair of white pleated pants that accommodated her thickening figure.

Stephanie had just put on some lotion when the phone rang. She grabbed for it and clicked on immediately. It was Dr. Ganis's nurse, who indicated he had an opening at 11:00 a.m. if she could make it. Stephanie said she'd be there and hung up.

Things couldn't be working out better. She'd

planned to go into town, anyway, and buy some picture albums. While she was at it, she'd look for a handicraft store in order to start making a quilt for the baby. While Nikos did business, she intended to stay busy and not bother him.

Nikos had told her she could use the car. While she left him alone to work, she would carry on with her new life. Besides loving to explore new places, Stephanie liked to cook. She could shop for food and fix their meals from now on. This evening she planned to prepare a totally American meal and surprise him. She wanted to help him. There was no use kidding herself any longer. She loved him desperately.

Once Nikos had showered and shaved, he got dressed and walked down the hall. Just as he knocked on Stephanie's door, she stepped out of the bedroom and then collided, wringing a small cry from her. He grabbed her arms to steady her. To his surprise he saw her wince. Not only that, he noticed a slight bruise along her jaw that hadn't been there when she'd gone to bed last night.

"You've hurt yourself!"

She averted her eyes. "It's nothing." She tried to ease away, but he prevented her from walking out the door.

"What's wrong with your arms?"

"Not a thing."

"Since you're wearing long sleeves, I'll be the judge of that. Let me see." With care he pushed the sleeve of her blouse up her right arm, but found nothing. When he did the same thing to the left, it was a tug-of-war, but he prevailed and saw bruising both above and below the elbow. "Who did this to you, Stephanie?"

"No one. When I was in the galley, I was clumsy getting something down from the cupboard. It hit my jaw and jammed my arm against the counter by accident."

"I don't believe you. Look at me." When she refused, he said, "These marks were made by someone's hand. You're trembling. Tell me the truth."

Finally, she lifted her eyes to him. Those dark blue pools stared at him in pain. "About three-thirty this morning I heard moaning sounds coming from the deck and thought it was an animal. When I went up to see…"

Nikos drew in a burning breath. "You found *me.*"

"Yes. I knelt down to try and comfort you."

He raked a hand through his hair, gutted to think she'd seen him like that and he didn't even remember it. "I could have done real damage to you and the baby. I could have given you a permanent injury, or worse!"

"But you didn't, Nikos. You were jerking, but you weren't violent and didn't walk around. Mostly you were crying Kon's name. I wouldn't have let myself get close to you otherwise."

"I should have told you about my PTSD. The doctor gave me medicine, but sometimes the nightmares come on, anyway. By not saying a word to you, I put you at risk and have done the unforgivable."

"That's not true!" She cupped his face between her hands. "I'm glad I saw you like that. It helped to understand what you've been going through since the explosion. You've suffered so terribly. All I wanted to do was calm you down." She kissed his lips. "After a little while you started to sleep peacefully again. I sat there until Yannis came on board."

Nikos backed away from her. "Forgive me."

"For deserting me on our wedding night?" she teased.

"You know what I mean." He rapped out the words angrily.

"Nikos, there's nothing to forgive. Now that I know, I have a suggestion, because I'm worried about you sleeping up on deck when one of those flashbacks hits. As you told me on the way out of the church, I'm your wife now, for better or worse, so why don't we sleep in the room with the twin beds? That way we can keep an eye on each other. When you have a bad night, you'll be safe and so will I."

"I'm not safe to be around anyone, especially not you when you're pregnant."

"Where did you get an idea like that? Thousands of soldiers come home from war with battle fatigue. They resume their lives with their wives, who are pregnant or not, and they work things out. To be honest, I asked Yannis for the name of your doctor this morning. I have an appointment at eleven. I'd like to hear what he has to say, and want you to come with me. But if you won't, I'm going anyway, because I need to know the best way to help you."

She headed for the galley. Nikos followed her and watched her reach for a roll. She darted him a glance. "Have you had breakfast?"

"I couldn't." He wasn't able to tolerate the thought of food after what he'd done to her. "Stop being so damn brave."

"That's what I've wanted to say to you since I saw that cane you've refused to use in front of me. Why don't we agree that *you've* tried to be brave long enough? Now it's time for us to be totally honest with each other. Otherwise how are we ever going to get through the rest of this pregnancy without losing our minds?"

Totally honest?

Since Stephanie had shown up on board the *Dio-medes,* he wasn't sure he was in control of his mind or his fears. Deep down he wanted the baby to be his more than anything in this world.

She poured herself a glass of orange juice and drank it. "I'm planning to do some grocery shopping while we're in town."

"We just stocked up a few days ago."

"Have you forgotten you've picked up an American wife since then? She'd like to make you some of her favorite foods." He blinked. "Oh, and will you bring the camera? We can take it to a print shop and have the pictures downloaded so we can mount them."

He cocked his head, amazed by this unexpected domestic side of her. Being with Stephanie on vacation hadn't prepared him for this aspect of her. "Anything else?"

She flashed him a full, unguarded smile that knocked him sideways, though the sight of the bruise on her jaw tortured him. "Since we don't know the gender of the baby yet, I think I'll work up a white puffy quilt and stencil it with the outline of a lamb. I'd love your input on the materials."

She washed out her glass in the sink. "I'll get my purse and see you at the car. If not, would you give me the keys?"

He ground his teeth. "I'm coming with you." As they left for town it occurred to him he needed to buy them a house, preferably today. The yacht was a great place for him to do business with Tassos, but it was no place for a woman whose nesting instincts had already kicked in.

While Nikos waited for her outside the local photo shop, he called Tassos, who knew of a villa he'd had in mind for Nikos for a while. It was in a more exclusive area of town that would be perfect for them.

With a phone call to a friend who was a Realtor, he made the arrangements and gave Nikos the address. The man agreed to meet Nikos and Stephanie there at one o'clock. That would give them enough time to see the doctor first.

It seemed to make Dr. Ganis's day to find out Nikos was married to a wife who intended to be proactive over his PTSD. He gave them a card they should both read regularly, but all the time he spoke, he couldn't take his eyes off her.

Nikos had already come to learn that with Stephanie's blond beauty and lithe figure, taking her out in public was proving to be a hazard. He could already count one traffic accident because the male driver had taken one look at her and driven right into the back of another car. It served the poor devil right.

Nikos read what was on the card.

Always be truthful with your vet, always keep safety in mind. Don't walk on eggshells. Grieve for what is lost and move on. Stay on top of medications. Short periods of withdrawal to help control anger make sense, but withdrawing from life into a "bunker" is not helpful. Conflict is normal. Focus on the issue at hand and resist bringing up

*issues from the past. Exercise, get regular meals,
good nutrition, plenty of rest and time for play.
Enjoy the good times. When bad times come, hang
on. Good times will come again.*

As they got up to leave his office, Stephanie won
the doctor over with her final comment. "I consider
these bruises *my* mark of bravery." His laughter followed them out the door.

Unable to help himself, Nikos gave her waist a
squeeze as they left the clinic for the car. "Do you mind
if we put off all the shopping until tomorrow? I have
a surprise for you that could take up most of our day.
Let's grab a bite to eat before we meet Mr. Doukakis."

Stephanie couldn't imagine what it was. However, she
was so happy to see that Nikos had forgiven himself
for the bruises, and seemed to be in a mellower mood,
that she didn't care what they did as long as it was together. When he'd interrogated her in the doorway of
her bedroom earlier that morning, she'd been frightened that irreparable damage had been done to their
relationship.

At one of the sidewalk cafés she ordered a lime
crush drink and discovered she adored the bruschetta
made with apple and goat cheese. Nikos downed a
whole loaf of lamb rolled slices. Taking the doctor's
advice, he passed on caffeine-laden coffee and ordered
decaf. Stephanie made a mental note to buy the same,
so he would sleep better.

When she couldn't eat another bite, he drove them
up a hillside covered with flowering vegetation. They
came to a charming, two-story villa, where he stopped

behind the car parked in front. The man at the wheel had to be this Mr. Doukakis he'd mentioned.

She flicked a glance at Nikos's striking profile. "What are we doing?"

He shut off the engine and turned to her. "Hoping to buy us a house."

What? "But I thought—"

"Let's not go there." He cut her off. "I'll use the yacht for business, but decorating one of the rooms below deck for a nursery is absurd."

"I agree, and have no intention of doing any such thing. As for the quilt, it'll be a gift for our baby. I'm looking forward to making it, that's all."

"You're avoiding the issue, Stephanie, and I know why. If you don't like the looks of this house, we'll find something better."

Just when she'd been on a real high, he'd sprung this on her. Already she could see the writing on the wall. While she was at the house, he'd work late, then call to tell her he was staying on the yacht overnight. No way!

"I don't want a house, not with you coming and going when the mood takes you."

"You mean you don't like *this* one," he thundered. "If you want a mansion, just say so and I'll accommodate you."

Now *she* was angry. "I thought we left that issue in the past, but I can see you won't let it go, about me wanting to marry you for your money. For your information, I *love* living on the water."

She watched his hands grip the wheel tighter. "It's no place for a baby."

"The baby won't be here for months! Why did you bother to marry me, Nikos? Sticking me in a house will make me feel like a kept woman. I thought you'd been honest with me, but you weren't."

His features had turned into a dark mask of anger. Good!

"Since it obviously irritates you to have a woman around, I'll settle for living on my own boat, to stay out of your way. Instead of a house, buy me one of those little one-person sailboats bobbing at the marina on Egnoussa. I'll pay you as much as I can when the condo sells."

"Don't say another word, Stephanie."

"You started this, so I'll say what I like. It would cost only a fraction of what it would take to buy me a mansion I don't want to live in by myself. Or better yet, let me *rent* a sailboat. That would be fair. Yannis could take me to pick one out, and bring it across to moor by the yacht. 'His and hers.' We'll be the talk of the island."

While she was still shaking from their angry clash, he got out of the car and walked to the other one. The two men spoke for a few minutes before Nikos came back and levered himself into the front seat once more.

She sensed he'd love to wheel away on screeching tires, but he controlled himself on the drive back to the dock. By the time they reached the parking area, she'd repented of the way she'd blown up at him.

The doctor's advice came to mind. Conflict was normal. Focus on the issue at hand, not past issues.

"Wait, Nikos," she said as he opened the door. "I apologize for my behavior. Instead of welcoming your gift, I threw it back in your face. I'm so sorry. Please forgive me."

He shifted his gaze to her. "I should have prepared you for what I had in mind."

She shook her head. "I'm afraid my reaction would have been the same. Look, I realize you were happy living by yourself on the yacht with Yannis. Then I came along and disturbed your world. If I promise not to be a nuisance or get in your way, can we start over? But I can't just be a lump around here. Give me a job and I'll do it, besides my share of the cleaning."

One dark brow lifted. "You really want to cook?"

"Yes. As many meals as you'll let me."

"Then so be it. That'll free up me and Yannis to do other work." Nikos closed the door. "Let's drive to the market. Ever since you mentioned American food, I've been relishing the thought of it."

Stephanie sighed in relief that they'd survived another skirmish. "Thank you. I promise you won't regret this."

Following her fried chicken for dinner that evening, both men finished off the apple pie. The fact that there were no leftovers told her she'd hit a home run on her first try.

Yannis got up from the table and winked at her. "If all your meals are this good, I'm going to put on weight."

"I'm glad you liked it."

After he disappeared, Nikos sat back in his chair with the hint of a smile. "I guess you know you're permanently hired. I'd help you with the dishes, but we're headed for Engoussa right now. I need to assist Yannis."

"Do you have business there?"

"Yes. I want my parents to meet you tonight."

Her heart started racing. "Do they know about us?"

"Not yet. I phoned and told them I'd be coming by. They'll send a car. It's time they met their daughter-in-law, before the news of our wedding reaches them."

The surprising revelation filled Stephanie with ambiguous feelings, of relief that their secret would be out, and anxiety because she wanted to make a good impression for Nikos's sake. "I'll wear the long-sleeved blouse with one of my new skirts."

He nodded his dark head. "Stephanie..." The way he said her name made her think he was dead serious. "Follow my lead and don't let my father intimidate you."

After Nikos left the galley, she put their plates in the dishwasher, already feeling intimidated. She wished she knew what kind of deep-seated trouble lay between Nikos and his father. If he'd just given her a hint...

She dressed for the evening, then waited up on deck as the yacht pulled up alongside the dock on Egnoussa. Fairyland at night. Few people were out.

Nikos joined her, looking fabulous in a silky black shirt toned with dark gray trousers. To her surprise he'd brought his cane. This was a first. Using it for support, he reached out with his free hand and grasped hers. They left the yacht and started walking along the pier, toward a black car she could see waiting in the distance.

It appeared the ordeal he was about to face had drained him physically. Stephanie would do everything in her power to help him. As they reached the car, she gave his hand a squeeze. But whatever his reaction might have been was lost when a stunning dark blond woman with appealing brown eyes opened the door and stepped out of the driver's seat.

"Nikolaos. It's been such a long time."

"Natasa." He let go of Stephanie's hand long enough to kiss the woman on both cheeks. "I didn't know you were on the island."

Stephanie felt de trop. This was the woman he would probably have married if Fate hadn't stepped in to change his life.

"When I heard you were coming, I arrived early and asked your parents if I could meet you at the dock so we could talk in private. They assumed you'd be alone. Who's your friend?"

Nikos turned to Stephanie. "This is Stephanie Walsh from Florida, in the States. She arrived a few days ago. Stephanie? This is Natasa Lander, an old friend."

"How do you do, Ms. Lander."

In the semidark, Natasa's face lost color. "Ms. Walsh," she acknowledged. "How is it you know Nikos?"

Stephanie groaned inwardly for this poor woman, who'd carried a torch for him all these years. It was no wonder. How could any other man compare?

"I was on a scuba diving vacation in the Caribbean months ago and we met."

"Why don't I drive?" Nikos offered. "When we reach the house, we can all catch up on each other's news at once."

Nikos... This was a terrible idea, but what could she do? While he helped Natasa into the backseat, Stephanie grabbed his cane and hurried around to the front to get in. As far as she was concerned, this was worse than any nightmare.

En route, Nikos chatted with Natasa the way you'd do with an old friend, drawing her out, until they reached the impressive Vassalos mansion with its cream-and-beige exterior. His ancestral home stood near the top of the hill next to equally imposing ones Stephanie had seen on her first day here. The burnt-orange-tiled roofs added a certain symmetry that gave the town its charm.

He pulled the car around to the rear and parked. Both Stephanie and Natasa moved quickly, not waiting for his help. Natasa went in the rear entrance first. Stephanie handed Nikos his cane, but he put it back in the car, then reached for her hand.

"Ready?" he asked under his breath. That forbidding black glitter in his eyes had returned. It was clear he hadn't been expecting Natasa. Stephanie suspected the other woman's appearance had been orchestrated by Nikos's father. Yet unseen, the older man made an adversary that caused the hairs on the back of her neck to stand up.

When she nodded with reluctance, she heard his sharp intake of breath. "Maybe this will help." He pulled her into his arms and found her mouth, kissing her with a fierceness she wasn't prepared for, almost as if he was expecting her to fight him.

Stephanie clung to him, helpless to do anything else, and met the hunger of his kiss with an eagerness she would find embarrassing later. At last he was giving her a husband's kiss, hot with desire, the one she'd been denied last night. Whether he was doing this to convince himself he was glad he hadn't married Natasa, she didn't know. But right now she didn't care.

The way he was kissing her took her back to that unforgettable night on the island, when they'd given each other everything with a matchless joy she couldn't

put into words. He pressed her against the doorjamb
to get closer. One kiss after another made her crazy
with desire. Stephanie was so in love with Nikos that
nothing existed for her but to love him and be loved.

All of a sudden she heard a man's voice delivering
a volley of bitter words in Greek. It broke the spell.
Gasping for breath, she put her hands against Nikos's
chest. He was much slower to react. Eventually, he let
her go, with seeming reluctance.

Still staring at her, he said, "Good evening, Papa.
Stephanie and I will be right in. Give us a minute more,
will you?"

Another blast of angry words greeted her ears.

"She doesn't speak Greek, Papa."

"How dare you bring this gold digging American
into our home!"

That was clear enough English for Stephanie, who
was thankful Nikos was still holding her. She eyed his
father covertly. Except for their height, the formidable
older man with gray hair didn't look like Nikos.

"I dare because she's my wife. We were married in
a private church service yesterday. I wanted you to be
the first to know."

"Then we'll get it annulled," he answered, without
taking a breath.

"Not possible, Papa. Father Kerykes officiated. Naturally, I expect you and Mother to welcome Stephanie
into the family. If you don't, then you'll never be allowed to see your grandchild."

Stephanie could hardly breathe. Nikos was claiming their child as his own even though he didn't have
proof?

"So you *are* pregnant!" his father virtually snarled

at her. "I told Nikos I suspected as much when I heard you'd come to Egnoussa to track him down. Trying to pass off your baby as my son's? There's a word for a woman like you."

The man had just provided part of the source for Nikos's basic distrust of her. She eased away from him and stared at his dad without flinching. "I'm sorry you feel that way, Mr. Vassalos. I've been anxious to meet the father of such a wonderful, honorable man. You're both very lucky. I never knew my father.

"But I have to say I'm sad you're on such bad terms. Our baby is going to want to know its grandparents. I can only hope that one day you'll change your mind about me enough to allow us into your life. Now if you'll excuse me, I'm going to wait in the car while Nikos spends some time with you and your wife. *Kalinihta.*"

Good night was one of the few words in Greek she'd picked up, from listening to Nikos and Yannis.

No sooner had she climbed in the front seat and shut the door than Nikos joined her behind the wheel. He didn't speak the whole time they drove to the port. Stephanie knew better than to talk, but her heart was heavy for him and the tragic situation with his father.

After he pulled around to the parking area of Vassalos Shipping, Nikos left the keys on the floor of the car and they walked back to the yacht. "I want to get to know your family, Nikos, but I couldn't possibly stay in their house, since it would cause too much stress for everyone.

"Much as I want to make things right, I can't tolerate your father's attitude or the way he spoke about me.

Maybe in time things will get better. I could hope for that, but not right now. I trust you understand."

Silence followed her remarks, until he helped her step on the deck. "I owe you an explanation."

She threw her head back, catching sight of his tormented expression. "If you mean that kiss you gave me at the back door was supposed to be an in-your-face gesture for your father's digestion, I already got the message."

"If you think that, you couldn't be more wrong," Nikos grated. "Just when I thought my father had run out of tricks, there he was once again, trying to set me up with Natasa. But this time you were there. No amount of makeup could conceal the bruise on your jaw. It stood out in the moonlight, reminding me that you'd unwisely faced my demons and held me during the night, despite the consequences to you and the baby.

"Tonight I realized how very beautiful you are and how courageous to have forgotten yourself to help me. No one has ever been that self-sacrificing for me. In a rush of emotion I felt the need to show you how I felt. Since my father chose that moment to appear, then he has to live with that picture, because I refuse to apologize for something that had nothing to do with him."

Stephanie swallowed hard. Nikos's sincerity defeated her. "Do you think Natasa saw us?"

He gave an elegant shrug of his shoulders. "If she did, let's hope it was cathartic."

For the other woman's sake, Stephanie hoped so, too, and looked away. "I would have liked to have met your mother."

"One day I'll introduce you to her and the whole family. They're very nice people."

One day. That sounded so lonely.

"Nikos...about the baby—"

The mere mention of it brought a look of anxiety to his dark eyes. "Are you all right?"

"I'm fine!" she assured him, not wanting to add to his worries. "I was just surprised you told your father."

Nikos's hard body tautened. "Hearing the truth from my lips has put an end to his dream of my marrying Natasa in order to consolidate our families. He's been stuck in that groove for a decade. Since I've refused to work in the company, he has lost his hold on me."

Stephanie drew closer to him. "What's he afraid of?"

Nikos studied her for a long moment. "At one time he thought I was Costor Gregerov's son."

It took a second for Stephanie's brain to compute. When it did, she let out a gasp. "Your mother and Kon's father?" Surely she'd misunderstood.

"It's complicated. My mother and Kon's mother were best friends growing up on Oinoussa. My parents married first and had two children before I came along. But Tiana's eventual marriage to Costor brought a lot of grief to her family, because he's part Turkish.

"In some corners of society, the Greeks and Turks refuse to mix. The built-in prejudice against him caused a painful division. For Tiana, it was she against the world once she'd married Costor. They had four children before Kon came along."

As Nikos peeled back the layers, Stephanie's anguish for his pain grew.

"My mother defended Tiana's decision and was always sympathetic to Costor. At one point someone started a rumor that she got too close to him. It wasn't true, and both my mother and Costor always denied it, but my father was a bigoted man. He believed it and there was an ugly falling out that never healed."

Stephanie bit her lip. "DNA testing wasn't available when you were born."

"No, but it wasn't needed. As Tiana once told me, the stamp of a Vassalos was unmistakable. Unfortunately, my parents' marriage suffered. It's a miracle my mother didn't leave him, but she loves him. She remained close friends with Tiana, which threw me and Kon together, but the damage done to both families during those early years was incalculable."

Stephanie clutched the railing. "What a tragedy."

Nikos nodded. "My father became controlling and possessive. He tried to rule my life and choose my associates, making sure I didn't mix with people like Kon's family. By my teens he'd cultivated a friendship with the Lander family, laying the groundwork for the future he envisioned for me. But he went too far when I was forbidden to spend any more time with Kon, who'd become like a brother to me. Naturally, I defied my father, because Kon had done nothing wrong."

Stephanie darted him a glance. "Except to be a constant reminder of the past."

Nikos breathed deeply. "Everything reached a boiling point when Kon needed money for his divorce. I gave him what I'd saved from working. My father found out and threatened to disown me. I told him it wouldn't be necessary, because Kon and I had already joined the navy and would be shipping out."

The night breeze had sprung up, lifting the hair off Stephanie's cheek. "You and Kon shouldn't have had to suffer for your father's paranoia. How long did it take him to beg your forgiveness?"

"His pride won't allow him to beg. For my mother's sake I visited them on leave, but things have never been the same. Underneath he's still a bigot and distrustful."

"Evidently he doesn't like Americans, either," she whispered.

"He's predisposed to dislike anyone whom he imagines might have control over me. I invested my military pay and bought the *Diomedes* so I would never have to be beholden to him."

Heartsick for Nikos, Stephanie looked at her husband through new eyes. Here she'd suffered all her life, wishing she knew anything about her father, while Nikos... Her ache for him grew worse. "I can't tell you how sorry I am."

"You've married into a complicated family. Don't try to sort it all out tonight. You look tired, which comes as no surprise after your wrestling match with me last night."

Stephanie would do it again and again if he'd let her, but after this incident with his father, she sensed he was unreachable. True enough, his next words left her in no doubt.

"You go below. I'll stay up here and wait for Yannis. As soon as he comes, we'll leave port and head back to Oinoussa."

CHAPTER EIGHT

September 1

NIKOS HAD SEEN his wife in a bikini when they swam on one of the isolated beaches. Oftentimes Elianna came with them. With the growing evidence of her pregnancy, there'd been a decided change in her since April, when they'd met. But he broke out in a cold sweat as he watched the doctor spread the gel on Stephanie's tummy to do a Doppler ultrasound.

"Ooh, that's cold."

"All my patients say that."

"Are you all right?"

"Of course she is." Dr. Panos smiled at Nikos. "Sit down, Kyrie Vassalos, and watch the screen. We'll take a peek inside to see how your baby is progressing. This will take about ten minutes."

Nikos couldn't sit. More than his concern about the gender of the baby was the fear that something might show up to indicate a problem. The doctor moved the probe over her belly. Pretty soon the sound of a heartbeat filled the examination room.

"Can you hear that?" Stephanie cried in excitement.

"Your baby has a good, strong heartbeat. Keep watching the screen."

Whether it was his baby or not, Nikos stood there mesmerized by the sight of pictures that gave evidence of the living miracle growing inside her.

The doctor nodded. "I like what I see."

"Then it's healthy?" Stephanie's anxious question echoed that of Nikos.

"At this stage everything looks fine and normal. The baby could fit in the palm of your hand."

Yet you could see it was a perfect baby. Nikos could only shake his head in awe.

"But it needs to turn for me if we're going to find out its gender." Dr. Panos pressed in various spots. "I know you're uncomfortable after drinking all that water, Stephanie. Just a few more minutes, then you can use the bathroom."

She let out a big sigh. "As long as there's nothing wrong, I don't care if it's a boy or a girl."

Since the night she'd held him during a flashback, Nikos had secretly worried he might have damaged the baby in some way. At the good news, exquisite relief swamped him.

Though she'd promised not to come near him at night, that fear had caused him to lock his bedroom door when he went to bed so she wouldn't try to help him during an episode. Much as he desired sleeping with her, even if it would only be in the cabin with twin beds, he didn't dare.

"From the positioning, I don't know if we're going to be successful. I need a better angle. Otherwise we could try another one in eight more weeks, at the end of your second trimester." He continued to move the probe. "This one is active and kicking."

"That sounds good to me," Stephanie told the doctor. "I want to teach it to scuba dive."

"So you're a diver."

"We both are," Nikos volunteered.

After a surprisingly long period of silence, Dr. Panos said, "Then let's hope he shares your interest."

"He?" they exclaimed in unison.

"See that?" He pointed to the baby's anatomy. "There's your boy. Got a name for him yet?"

Her eyes filled with tears as she looked at Nikos. "Nikolaos Alexandros Vassalos!"

Stephanie...

Dr. Panos chuckled. "Well, that sounded definite." He turned off the machine and handed each of them a photo. "You can get up and use the restroom now. Keep taking your iron and vitamin pills, get plenty of rest, and I'll see you in a month. Make your appointment with my receptionist on your way out."

"Thank you!" Stephanie murmured emotionally.

"You're entirely welcome. Congratulations."

Nikos shook his hand, then studied the pictures while he waited for her. He couldn't help remembering the time in the hospital when he'd been told he would never father a child, would never know the joy of hearing those words from a doctor, let alone be given pictures.

Stephanie's glowing face was the first thing he saw when she met him out in reception. With excitement she scheduled her next visit, for early October.

Don't let your doubts drag you down now, Vassalos.

He ushered her outside to the parking lot. "This calls for a celebration. What would you like to do?"

"Go to a furniture store and buy a crib. I've almost finished the lace edge on the quilt and can't wait to see it set up in my room."

"Be honest with me, Stephanie. Wouldn't you rather we went looking for a house first?"

His question brought shadows to her eyes. "I thought we went through this a month ago."

"I was afraid you were humoring me. I thought to give you a little more time."

She put her hands on her hips. "I think it's time you were honest with me. Are you dying to live in a house? Or have you decided you want to deposit me in one before you go crazy? I'm getting the message you need space away from me, while you conduct your business meetings on board. If that's the case, please say so now."

"Space is not the issue."

Color tinted her cheeks. "Then what is?"

"I was only thinking of your happiness while you make preparations for the baby that's coming."

"I'm perfectly happy, but apparently you're not. So I have an idea. While I go back to the yacht, you can look at furnished homes to your heart's content with Mr. Doukakis. Let me know when you find the one you think will suit me best, and I'll move into it."

Damn. On this red letter day he'd mentioned a house only to please her, not to undo all the joy she'd been feeling since her visit to the doctor.

"Not every woman with a baby coming wants to live on the water."

"But I'm not every woman," she retorted. "The yacht

is home to me. From my condo I used to watch ocean-going vessels out on the water and dream about sailing around the world on one. That idea has always intrigued me."

He nodded. "Then I won't mention buying a home again. After we find the right crib, let's have lunch on the island before we return to the *Diomedes*."

Now that she had run out of steam, she seemed to droop a little. "Nikos? Forgive me for snapping at you. I can't believe I talked to you like that when you're always so wonderful to me. The truth is I've been so happy, I haven't wanted anything to change. But that's the selfish part of me talking. I'll go with you to look at a house, and never complain again. The last thing I want to be is a carping wife." Her voice caught.

"Carping?"

"Yes, as in a petty woman who looks for trouble and finds fault at every turn, appreciating nothing. With your command of English, I'm surprised you haven't heard that word."

He cradled her lovely face in his hands, forcing her look at him. She'd picked up a golden glow since living on the yacht. Her eyes shimmered an intense blue. Nikos could easily get lost in them. "You're none of those things and you know it."

"I'm the ball on your chain, holding you back." She was serious.

Laughter rose out of his throat. "From what?"

She averted her eyes. "From whatever you planned to do before I ventured into Vassalos territory without permission. I look back on it now and can't believe I was so audacious."

Right now he couldn't relate to the man who'd

collided with her along the pier. That man had been
drowning in despair, without a glimmer of hope. For
a moment he'd thought he was hallucinating. But the
minute he'd touched her, he'd realized she was no figment of his imagination. Stephanie Walsh had mate-
rialized in the flesh.

Nikos slid his hands to her shoulders, covered by
her leaf-green top. His fingers played with the ends of
her silvery-gold hair. Desire for his pregnant wife was
eating him alive. Oh yes, she was pregnant. He had the
proof resting in his pocket.

With their mouths so close, it was all he could do not
to devour her in front of the people coming and going
from the clinic. But he did kiss her very thoroughly,
and was shaken by her powerful response.

"I dare you to kiss me like that when we're back on
the yacht and no one is watching," she teased.

That's what drew him to Stephanie. Though she
could be fiery, she didn't take herself too seriously, and
retained a sense of humor lacking in the women he'd
known. They'd had a month of togetherness and he still
wasn't tired of her. If anything, he couldn't wait to get
her back to the yacht. He'd taken the day off work and
no one else would be around.

"I'm so glad you know how to put this crib together.
I wouldn't have a clue." Stephanie sat propped on her
bed, finishing the lace edge of the baby quilt while she
watched her husband work. As she studied his dark,
handsome features, a feeling of contentment stole
through her.

She picked up the ultrasound picture and studied it
for the hundredth time. Knowing she was carrying his

son made this day unforgettable. How could Nikos possibly not know and feel that this was *his* baby?

But every time she put herself in his shoes, she remembered the horror story about his parents. And not just his parents, but the tragic lie that had bound Kon to the Frenchwoman. Trust was one of the most vital essentials in a relationship, let alone a marriage. Nikos's view of life and women had been flawed because of circumstances, yet there was a part of him that was still giving her a chance. She loved him for that modicum of trust in her, loved him with every fiber of her being.

"It's your fault I feel stuffed after eating lunch." It had been a marvelous lunch of filet of sole with grapes and capers. "I've gained too much weight since my first doctor's appointment, in Florida. Do you realize there's no such a thing as a bad meal on Oinoussa?"

He darted her an all-encompassing glance that sent a shiver of excitement through her body. "Nor on the *Diomedes*. The acquisition of my new cook is putting back the pounds I lost in the hospital. When we were on the island, you never told me you're such a fabulous cook."

"You and Yannis are full of it, but it's nice to hear. Mom was always at work, so my grandmother taught me a lot of her recipes."

"Yannis says you put Maria's cooking to shame."

"It's the butter instead of the olive oil."

"I like both."

"So do I. The blending of two worlds." She let out a sigh. "Nikos? I've started picking up some Greek around you and Yannis, but it's a slow process. I want to be able to talk to the baby in both languages. How would you feel if I found someone on Oinoussa to tutor me for a few hours every day? You speak perfect English. I feel embarrassed that I can't converse in Greek."

"I think it's an excellent idea."

"You do?" She'd been holding her breath in case he told her the future was still uncertain and he didn't think it was necessary.

"I'll look into it." On that satisfying note he got to his feet. "The crib is finished. What do you think?" He'd placed it against the wall opposite the end of her bed.

"I love it! I'm glad we picked the walnut for Alex." She rolled off the bed. Together they added the mattress and padding. When she'd fastened the ties, she reached for the baby quilt and spread it along the railing.

Nikos examined the hand stitching. "You do perfect work. Anyone would think you'd bought this. I'm more impressed than I can say."

"It's full of mistakes, but thanks. I hope he has your black hair. Against the white material, he'll be gorgeous. I can't wait to wrap him in it."

In the next breath Nikos pulled it off the railing and wrapped it around her neck and shoulders. "If he has your blond hair, the effect with this quilt will be sensational." Still holding the material, Nikos drew her close. "All his friends will say he has the most beautiful mother in the Oinousses."

"*Nikos, I—*"

The rest of her words were smothered as he claimed her mouth and slowly savored her as if she were something fragile and precious. Heat began to course through her body, making her legs tremble. She slid her hands up his chest, where she could feel the solid pounding of his heart beneath his sport shirt. For so long Stephanie had been waiting for a sign that he still wanted her. Her great need caused her to respond with an ardor she didn't know herself capable of.

He picked her up and laid her on the bed before stretching out next to her. "Today when I saw the doctor spread the gel and use the probe, I wanted to be the one to feel the baby, Stephanie. Let me feel you now." His voice throbbed.

She responded with a moan as he lifted the hem of her blouse and pulled down the elasticized waist of her skirt. When his hand moved over her belly, sensation after physical sensation swept through her. "Our baby is right there."

As he lowered his mouth to the spot, the shock of his kiss traveled through her womb. Stephanie was filled with indescribable delight and the hope that everything was going to be all right. She let out a helpless cry and once again their mouths sought each other and clung.

There were so many things she'd been wanting to tell him. Now she could show him, without words getting in the way. She'd thought she'd loved him before, but after living together for a month her feelings for him had deepened in new ways and had taken root.

"Don't be afraid you're going to hurt me," she begged, wanting him to crush her in his arms. Though she sensed his growing desire, he held back, kissing her with tenderness rather than the kind of passion she'd once known with him. She wanted more.

He buried his face in her neck. "I don't want to do anything that could injure the baby."

Surely he knew that couldn't happen. Or was he covering for something else she'd secretly worried about from the moment he'd told her he was sterile? "There's no fear of that, unless it's your own injury stopping you."

Nikos lifted his head and looked down at her in confusion. "What do you mean?"

"I'm talking about the deep bruising to your spine from the explosion. When you push yourself too hard, I can tell when you're in pain, but I'm wondering if it's more than that."

To her chagrin he rolled off the bed and got to his feet. "Explain what you mean."

Stephanie sat up, furious with herself for ruining the moment. "I've wondered if your PTSD wasn't the only reason you didn't want to sleep with me in the cabin with the twin beds. If you can't make love, then please tell me. Don't you know it could never matter to me?"

He reared his head in obvious surprise. "There's nothing wrong with me in that department."

For a moment she couldn't breathe, she was so thrilled to hear that news, for his sake. "I—I'm sorry if I jumped to the wrong conclusion," she stammered. "Thank heaven you're all right."

But another part of her was humiliated to have given herself away. It meant he had another reason for not making love to her. Afraid she knew what it was, she got off the bed and put the fallen quilt back on the crib railing.

"Looking back on the explosion, I suppose you could say the collateral damage didn't take everything away," he murmured.

Needing to do something to deflect the pain after that grim assessment, she started cleaning up the mess they'd made. He took the plastic from her hands. "I'll take care of this."

Unable to meet his gaze, she reached for a book she'd been reading, and hurried up on deck to put distance between them. Now that she knew the whole truth of their situation from her husband's lips, she could envision what life had been like after Nikos's father accused his mother of being unfaithful, all of it based on a vicious rumor. The thought that the baby might not be his had changed the dynamics of their marriage.

Was Nikos following the same pattern? Unsure of her still, would he go only so far and no further while he waited for the result in January?

Stephanie had thought her husband was beginning to believe their baby was his. A few minutes ago she'd felt closer to him than she'd thought possible. Though she could shout it to the heavens that the stamp of a Vassalos would be on their little boy, she would never be able to convince Nikos of it until after the delivery.

"Stephanie?"

She wheeled around just as she'd arranged a lounger to sit in while she read. "Yannis! I didn't know you were here. We thought you wouldn't be back until tonight."

"I've got some repair work to do and decided to get at it before dark."

Put on a good face.

She could tell he was dying to know how her doctor's visit went, but he was never one to pry into her business. "We got back a while ago. Nikos set up a crib in my room. You'll be impressed what a good job he did. Our baby boy will be very happy in it."

A grin broke out on the man's bronzed face. "You're going to have a son?"

"That's what the doctor said. We plan to call him Alex."

"That's a fine family name."

"Yes. Ask Nikos to show you a picture."

The older seaman's eyes looked suspiciously bright. "I'm very happy for you."

"We're happy, too." She would keep up the pretense if it killed her. "Thank you for all your kindness to me, Yannis. You do so many things to help me, and I'm grateful."

"It's my pleasure."

"Nikos couldn't get along without you, even if you do put him through torture every day helping him do his exercises. But you already know that, don't you?"

For once she saw him blush.

"He's a slave driver, all right." Nikos had just joined them. "I guess my wife has told you the news."

Yannis clapped him on the shoulder. "She says you have a photo."

"Right here." Nikos pulled it out of his pocket.

The seaman's eyes squinted against the light to get a good look. "He's beautiful, like his mother."

"I was just telling her he'll have the most beautiful woman on the island for his *mana.*"

But you can't take credit for being the father yet, her heart cried.

Stephanie would have to harden herself, because this was going to be the way of it for the next five months.

CHAPTER NINE

December 10

STEPHANIE LOVED HER Greek lessons. For the last four months Yannis had driven her faithfully to and from the school on Oinoussa every weekday after breakfast for her two-hour session with Borus. The forty-year-old was a part-time counselor who was glad for the extra money. He was also a lot of fun.

The closer she drew to her delivery date, the more taciturn and anxious Nikos had become. Whether or not he believed this child was his, she knew he worried. Even though Dr. Panos had assured him at every appointment that she was coming along normally, with no unexpected complications, he didn't seem to quite believe it, and hovered over her until there were times when she wanted to scream.

With the baby due in three weeks, he argued with her that she should stop the lessons. A month ago he'd told her no more swimming with Tassos's wife in order to give her scuba pointers.

While they were eating breakfast this morning, she asked Nikos if he was ordering her to stay home today. The question turned his features into a cool mask before he told her the lessons would end when her teacher left for the Christmas holidays on the seventeenth.

With that pronouncement Nikos got up from the table, taking his coffee with him to the lounge to work. These days the *Diomedes* stayed in port and he used a small cruiser to travel back and forth from the rig erected offshore.

To her joy his business with Tassos was growing, and he'd acquired rights to drill off some of the other uninhabited islands of the Oinousses cluster. His strong concern for the environment made certain there'd be no damage to the local habitat.

As usual when Stephanie came out of class, she tried out what she'd learned on Yannis, who was an excellent teacher himself. But today when he greeted her, she could tell he had something serious on his mind.

"What's wrong? Has something happened to Nikos?" she cried in alarm.

"No, no."

"Thank goodness." She had to wait for her heartbeat to slow down.

"You have a visitor on board. She's very anxious to talk to you."

Stephanie frowned. "Who?"

"Kyria Vassalos, Nikos's mother."

"Oh…" She couldn't believe it. "Is Nikos with her?"

"No. He's gone to the rig. She came when she knew he wouldn't be here."

"How did she know?"

"Because I worked for her when he was just a boy. We've always been friends."

"Which means you've always kept her informed." Stephanie got it.

"Yes. Today Nikos's father is away in Athens on business. It's been her first chance to come and visit. I sent my son to fetch her in his boat. But if you don't want to meet her, I'll tell her to go back to Egnoussa."

"No. Don't do that." More than anything in the world Stephanie had wanted to meet his mother. She just hadn't expected their first meeting to happen when she was in full bloom, with swollen feet and her face marked with chloasma, the pregnancy mask. If she could be thankful for one thing, it was that she could carry on a basic conversation in Greek.

Her nervousness increased as Yannis drove her to the port. Together they walked along the pier to the yacht. Stephanie could see his mother looking out from the rail. Her luxuriant black hair was pulled back in a stylish twist. She was trim, and shorter than Stephanie by several inches. With her white slacks and stunning blue blouse setting off her olive skin, she was a true Grecian beauty. This was where Nikos got his fantastic looks.

As Stephanie stepped on board, the older woman turned, focusing her soft brown eyes on her. "I hope you don't mind," she said in accented English. "I've wanted to meet the woman my son married. I'm sorry it didn't happen when you came to our home. You need to know I'm ashamed of my husband's behavior toward you. My name is—"

"Hestia." Stephanie supplied it for her. "I know your name and I'm so glad you're here now," she said in her best Greek. "You raised a wonderful son. I love him very much."

His mother made a quiet study of her. "For him to

have married you the day after you arrived in Greece, it's obvious how he feels about you."

Stephanie shook her head. "He married me for the sake of the baby." Taking a risk, she added, "He doesn't believe he's the father."

Hestia looked stunned. "I don't understand."

"Come downstairs with me and we'll talk." They went below. "Can I get you something to drink?"

"Nothing, thank you."

"Then come to my room."

A gasp escaped Hestia's lips when she saw the bedroom turned into a nursery. Between Stephanie's bed and everything a mother needed to take care of her new baby, there was barely room to move.

At this point Stephanie's speech was sprinkled with Greek and English. "Please sit down in the rocking chair. I have something to give you." She went over to the dresser and pulled out a photo album. "I wish you had been at the wedding. You should have been there. I made this for you and your husband to keep."

The older woman opened the cover. For the next five minutes she remained speechless as she looked at all the pictures. When she finally lifted her head, tears were rolling down her cheeks. Stephanie saw in those brown eyes all the sorrow a mother could at missing out on her child's wedding day.

"Nikos told me about your husband's distrust when you were pregnant with him. I'm afraid the same thing has happened to me. We had only ten days together on vacation last April. We don't know that much about each other, and so much happened after he had to return to active duty, it raised his doubts about life. About everything."

His mother nodded sadly. "Even though he could walk, he was on the verge of giving up when we took him home from the hospital."

Tears welled in Stephanie's eyes. "He's much better now, but he won't believe this is his baby until after Alexandros is born."

"You can forgive my son for this?"

She smiled. "Didn't you forgive his father?" Stephanie reached for the sonogram picture and showed it to her. "That was at four months. He was only four and half inches long. Now look at him." She placed her hands on top of her big stomach.

Hestia didn't give her a verbal answer, but got to her feet. After setting the album on the dresser, she put her arms around Stephanie and hugged her. "You must come for Christmas and stay the whole day. Everyone wants to meet you. I won't take no for an answer."

Stephanie's heart warmed. "We'll be there. Even if Nikos is still upset with his father, he won't dare refuse to accompany me if I go. He hovers around me constantly these days. Sometimes he follows me when I have to go to the bathroom!"

Laughter bubbled out of her mother-in-law. "That's how my husband was with all three of our children, doubts and all." She wiped her eyes. "I'm going to leave so Nikos won't find me here when he comes home."

"Yannis will see you out to the dock." Stephanie handed her the album to take with her.

"He's a treasure, but I'm sure you've learned that for yourself by now."

"Definitely."

"Take good care of yourself, Stephanie. Your time is close."

"Don't worry. Nikos does it for both of us."

They both laughed as they started up the stairs. Stephanie felt as if she was floating. Already she loved Nikos's mother.

December 17

Nikos lounged against the door of the car while he waited for Stephanie to come out of the school. After going to her doctor's appointment with her, he'd driven her straight here. He was glad this would be her last day of Greek lessons. Her due date was two weeks from tomorrow. Dr. Panos had told her to rest and keep her feet up. Nikos intended to see that she followed his instructions.

Just when his patience had worn thin and he was ready to go in and get her, the school doors opened and his wife emerged with her teacher. Borus Paulos had come highly recommended, but all Nikos could see was that he was enamored of her in the jacketed white sundress she'd bought that first day shopping.

The man gesticulated while he continued talking. Nikos doubted he'd noticed him waiting, but Stephanie saw him. She waved before saying goodbye to her teacher. Then she started walking toward him.

For a moment he was transported back to the Caribbean. He'd been walking along the beach with Angelo when he saw this woman in a wet suit with a fabulous body. Her hair looked gilded in the sun. She was coming to meet Angelo on those long, elegant legs.

When she drew closer, her gaze suddenly switched to Nikos. Her eyes were an impossible blue color, dazzling like rare gems. Her voluptuous mouth curved into a friendly smile. She looked happy and excited because they were going to dive. At that moment the most remarkable sensation had passed through Nikos's body and he was never the same again.

That same electrifying feeling was attacking him now as Stephanie approached the car and their gazes met. He lost his breath. This woman with child was his wife! Whether the baby was his or not, he realized it no longer mattered to him. Somehow over the months they'd become his family. If he'd seen this day while he lay recuperating in the hospital, he would have thought he'd lost his mental faculties along with the ability to walk.

"Sorry it took me so long to get away," she said a little breathlessly. "Borus is a talker when he gets going."

"It wasn't your fault." Her tutor couldn't help his hormones raging in her presence. In fact, the way Nikos himself was feeling at the moment, he didn't dare touch her while they were in front of other people. He opened the passenger door to help her in, seduced by the strawberry-scented shampoo she used in the shower. When her swollen belly brushed against him by accident, his heart gave an extra beat in wonder, while she let out a gentle laugh.

By some miracle she'd stayed incredibly healthy throughout her pregnancy. She'd never developed the serious problems he'd heard various married business associates talk about. Though she complained of swelling and the chloasma she insisted made her resemble a raccoon, he'd never seen her more beautifully feminine.

It had taken control almost beyond his endurance to stay away from her. Because of his injury she'd wrongly assumed he couldn't make love to her as he'd done on the island. But only one thing had held him back. Stark staring fear.

She didn't know what it was like to worry that he might cause harm to her and the baby during a flashback. It was the only force strong enough to keep him locked up in his room night after night. After living together this long without an incident that left bruises on her, he refused to allow anything to go wrong now.

After lunch they were going to do the last of their Christmas shopping. Just a few more presents, nothing taxing. While they were gone, he'd instructed Yannis to put up the little Christmas tree with lights he'd bought and smuggled on board. The lounge was the best place to surprise her. It wasn't a tradition Nikos followed, but he knew Americans were big on it, and such things were important to his wife.

He darted her a glance before he started the car. "Hungry?"

"You know, for once I'm not? But if you want to eat before we shop, that's fine with me."

"What I'd like to do is get the gift buying over with as fast as possible and go back home. I'll cook today and surprise you with something you haven't had before."

She smiled at him. "I'd love that."

"Good."

With the much cooler late autumn temperatures, she appeared to thrive. He could only marvel at her energy.

"Let's shop at the main department store," she suggested. "That way we can find everything we want under one roof."

"I was thinking the same thing." He headed in that direction. "Just so you know, Tassos phoned while I was waiting for you. He and Elianna have invited us to their house for their family's Christmas Day party."

He felt Stephanie stir restlessly in the seat. "That's very nice of them, but we can't go."

He frowned. "Why not?"

When she remained quiet, he slanted her a glance. "Stephanie? What's wrong?"

"Nikos," she began, but her hesitation was plain as day. He saw a guilty look enter her eyes. It surprised him no end.

"You don't want to go?"

"Under other circumstances I would, but that's not it." She shook her head. "I have a confession to make."

Just when he'd been thinking nothing had gone wrong with her pregnancy, he was terrified she was going to tell him something he didn't want to hear. On impulse he pulled over to the side of the street and shut off the engine. Turning in the seat, he slid his arm behind her and tugged on a few strands of her hair.

"Are you ill? Is there something you didn't tell the doctor this morning?"

"This isn't about me. I...it's about us."

In an instant his blood ran cold. "You mean after all this time, you've chosen today instead of Christmas to tell me who the father of your baby is?"

"No! Nikos." Her horrified cry reverberated in the car. "I'm going about this all wrong. Your mother came to see me last week while your father was away in Athens. We had a frank talk about everything. I showed her the sonogram picture. She's wonderful and I love her already. Before she left, I gave her the wedding album I made for them. She has invited us to spend Christmas Day with your family. I accepted for us."

After he'd imagined every horrific thing possible that could destroy life as he knew it, her explanation came as a complete shock. It took a minute for him to assimilate what she'd just said. He waited until he'd calmed down enough to talk. "That won't be a problem. I'll phone and tell her we've made other plans. She'll understand."

"No, I don't think she will. Nikos," Stephanie said in a tremulous whisper. "She adores you and needs to see her son. They've missed out on more than a decade of your life. You can't disappoint them. Life's too short."

He sucked in his breath. "My father's bias against Castor and his children for being who they are has been unconscionable, Stephanie. After what he did to my mother and the way he spoke to you, I can't be in the same room with him."

She put a hand to his cheek. "But she's forgiven him and so have I. As you told me, he's afraid and doesn't know how to make things right. If you don't show him the way, his fear of losing you will send him to the grave a desperately unhappy man. What joy could there be in that for any of us?"

Nikos felt sick to his stomach. "I can't do it. Don't ask that of me."

Stephanie pulled her hand away from him and stared out the window. "Then you go to Tassos's family for Christmas. I'll go to your parents and take your family their gifts."

Seeing black, Nikos started the car and drove straight to the dock.

As Stephanie passed the lounge on her way to the bedroom, she saw a five-foot Christmas tree studded with colored lights set up over by the entertainment center. Yannis had been busy while they'd been gone. She walked over to it and examined some of the ornaments.

After the devastating silence in the car while Nikos drove them back to the yacht, the sight of this brought her immeasurable delight. There was no one like Nikos. But the lights brought pain, too, making a mockery of the peace and joy Christmas was supposed to bring. They'd reached an impasse. His mother's invitation and Stephanie's acceptance had ruined this beautiful day.

Desperate to make things right between them, she hurried to his room before he could lock her out. That's what he'd been doing for months. The night before last she'd heard the gut-wrenching moaning and sobbing that came from his bedroom. So far she'd counted four episodes she knew about since their wedding.

When she discussed this with Yannis, the older man said it was a good sign that they weren't happening as often as they had in the beginning, which could only mean Nikos was slowly getting better. Stephanie wanted that for him more than anything.

He was such an outstanding man; she couldn't reconcile everything she knew about him with the side of his nature that had caused him to shut down just now. She couldn't leave it alone. This was too serious. Without knocking, she opened the door, determined they were going to talk everything out.

She couldn't prevent the cry that escaped when she discovered he'd removed his clothes and had just pulled on his black bathing trunks. With his back still to her, she saw the bruising at the lower part of his spine. Since he'd always worn his wet suit when they went swimming, she hadn't realized how deep and pervasive his injury had been. To think of his lying in that hospital bed broken and in despair… She couldn't bear it.

He wheeled around, a live, breathing, angry Adonis. That awful glittery look in his jet-black eyes impaled her, freezing the breath from her lungs. "I don't recall inviting you in here." The wintry tone he'd once used with her was back in full force.

Stephanie couldn't swallow. "I was afraid I might not get an invitation. I came in to tell you how sorry I am that I didn't let you know about your mother's visit until now. You've suffered years of pain over a situation I haven't fully comprehended until today. I'll call your mother and tell her we can't come."

It was as if he'd turned to stone. She couldn't reach him.

"I should never have attempted to tell you anything about your life or your thoughts," she went on. "I do have an audacious nature and realize it's a glaring flaw in my makeup. So I'll make you a promise now that I'll never keep anything from you again, or try to influence your thinking in any way. I swear it."

Desolate at this point because of his silence, she turned to leave, but paused in the doorway. "I love the Christmas tree. No woman in the world has a better husband than you. I'm sorry you can't say the same thing about your wife. To tell you I'm sorry I came to Greece would be a lie, but I'd give anything if I'd been honest with you after your mother left the other day. I've trespassed on your soul, Nikos. Forgive me. It will never happen again."

She rushed to her room and lay down on her back, pressing the pillow against her face to stifle her sobs. It wasn't long before she heard the familiar sound of

the cruiser. Who knew when Nikos would be back?
And when he did return, there was no guesstimating
how soon he'd speak to her again.

Stephanie knew he couldn't tolerate the sight of her
right now. She didn't blame him. That's why he'd taken
off. Perhaps the best thing to do was give him some
space. The more she thought about it, the more she
liked the idea. While she put a plan into action, she ate
a substantial lunch and made a phone call.

Once that was done she packed an overnight bag
with several days' worth of clothes. On her way out she
stopped in the lounge to put some presents under the
tree for Nikos. Presents made it look ready for Christmas. After that she wrote him a note, leaving it on his
desk where he would see it.

*Dear Nikos. We've been together constantly since
I barged into your life. What was it Kahlil Gibran
once wrote? "There should be spaces in your togetherness." I agree with his philosophy, so I'm
taking myself off until the day after Christmas.
Don't worry. I won't be far. Please be assured I
won't embarrass you by bothering anyone you
know or care about. Our business stays our business. I think you know I would never do anything
that put me or the baby in danger. I want Alex to
know his father. S.*

Nikos could be gone for the rest of the day. As for
Yannis, he'd said he'd be back at three. She had a half
hour to leave without him seeing her.

The town had only two taxis. One of them was waiting for her at the dock. She got in and told the driver

to drop her off on a corner where she'd seen used cars for sale. Her passport still showed she was single. The man who sold her the car had no idea she was Kyria Vassalos. That suited her fine. It didn't take long before she was in possession of a clunker that cost only five hundred dollars.

Free to do what she wanted, Stephanie drove to a wonderfully sited convent nestled among pines and ringed with a magnificent garden. The weary traveler was welcome to stay at their hospice, which was located on the west side of the island, about ten minutes from town. During one of their lessons Borus had told her she should visit to learn its history.

En route she passed several quiet coves, enchanted by the scenery and grateful she could use her bank card to draw money from her final paycheck. She still had enough to pay the fee for board and room for a week.

The convent suited her perfectly. For the time being she intended to get some reading done and keep her feet up. But when she got restless, she could take short drives around the island. It helped to know she'd be out of Nikos's hair for a while. He'd been hurtled into a world of pain after he'd left the Caribbean, and deserved a break.

As she'd told him, she was the ball on the end of his chain. By her staying here at the convent, out of sight, he didn't have to drag it around. For the time being he didn't know where to find her and that was good. He hovered too much.

On the plus side, she could give in to her emotions, which were out of control at this stage of her pregnancy. If she wanted to cry her heart out at night, no one would hear her through the thick walls.

Once in her simple room, she sank down on the bed.
Right now she was so exhausted she couldn't move.
For the last hour she'd had pain in her lower back. It
was from all the walking she'd done today. Tomorrow
she'd go out in the garden, but not now.

Evening had fallen before Nikos returned to the dock.
Yannis was waiting to help him tie up the cruiser. But
there was a worried look on the older man's face that
raised the hair on the back of Nikos's neck.

"Is Stephanie all right?"

"That's the problem, Nikos. I don't know. When I
came back at three she was gone, but she left a note on
the desk in the lounge."

Forgetting the pain in his back, Nikos raced along
the pier to the yacht and hurried down the stairs. As
he read her message, his heart plunged like a boulder
crashing down a mountain. "She had to have called for
a taxi to take her to one of the tourist lodgings. I'll call
and find out which one."

But when he finally reached the driver who'd picked
her up, the man was no help. "I dropped her off on a
corner by the Pappas Market. She was carrying an
overnight bag."

Searing pain ripped Nikos open before he hung up.
"I've got to find her tonight!"

Yannis looked grim. "You get dressed and we'll go
to every place where she might be staying."

Nikos changed into jeans and a sweater before they
took off for town in the car. They combed the whole
area for an hour, without results. "I should never have
closed up on her like I did earlier. She couldn't help it
that Mother came to see her."

"That was my fault, Nikos."

He stared hard at his friend. "No. The fault is all mine for letting old wounds fester until the result caused Stephanie to run away from me. I can't lose her, Yannis." His voice shook. "Where in the hell has she gone?"

"How did she find you?"

The shrewd seaman's question gave Nikos pause. He struggled for breath. "Through sheer persistence and determination." His mind reeled with possibilities. "Since she's not at any local lodgings, she had to get a ride with someone to somewhere else." His turmoil grew worse.

Yannis patted his shoulder. "Perhaps she went to another part of the island."

"Maybe. But there's no place for her to stay, only ruins and churches."

"Could she have gone back to the dock, to take the boat to Chios?"

"Anything's worth looking into." Nikos got the port authority on the line. The captain in charge of the last crossing was emphatic that a blonde, pregnant American woman had not been on board.

Nikos shook his head. "She's here somewhere, Yannis. Maybe she crept on some fishing boat down at the harbor to spend the night."

Yannis scratched his head. "I don't think she'd do that, not in her condition. She's so excited about that baby, she'd never put herself in precarious circumstances. Besides, everyone knows you. I doubt she'd do anything that could embarrass you. She said as much in the note."

Nikos stared blindly at the water in the distance.

"She had to get help from someone, but in my gut I know she wouldn't turn to Tassos or my family. She hasn't made any friends yet."

"That's not exactly true."

His gaze swerved to Yannis. "What do you mean?"

"Bulos."

Though she'd spent ten hours a week for months with her language teacher, Nikos still ruled him out and shook his head. "Let's go home and see if she's back on board the *Diomedes*. If not, I'll think about bringing in the police."

Except that she expected him to trust her enough to take care of herself and come back when she was ready. The police would want to know why she was missing and would figure out she and Nikos were having a domestic quarrel. It would be the talk of the Oinousses.

By three in the morning it was clear she wasn't coming back. Nikos thought he'd been at the end of his rope in the hospital, but this was agony in a new dimension. If anything untoward happened to her or the baby because of him, life wouldn't be worth living.

Yannis made them coffee. Both of them were too wired from anxiety to do anything but pace. They were waiting for morning so they could begin their search all over again.

At five to four Niko's cell phone rang, causing him to almost jump out of his skin. He clicked on. "Stephanie?"

"No, sir. This is Sister Sofia at the Convent of the Holy Virgin on Oinoussa. Are you Kyrie Vassalos?"

Beads of perspiration broke out on his forehead. "Speaking." He couldn't imagine why she'd called.

"Your wife checked into our hospice this afternoon."
The hospice! Of course! "But she's been in labor ever
since and is now at the hospital."

Nikos weaved in place. "God bless you, Sister.
You've just saved my life!" He hung up. "Yannis?
Stephanie is at the hospital having the baby!"

With Yannis driving, they made it there in record
time. Nikos burst inside the emergency entrance. "My
wife!" he said to the surprised attendant. "Stephanie
Vassalos—"

"She's in the delivery room."

"Has she had the baby?"

"Not yet. Dr. Panos says for you to come with me.
I'll get you ready. We need to hurry."

The next few minutes were a blur as Nikos was instructed to sanitize his hands before being led into the
delivery room. He was told to sit.

"Nikos!" He heard Stephanie call out to him.

"You're just in time," the doctor said without missing a beat. "Your baby fooled everyone and decided
to come a few weeks early. Push, Stephanie. That's it.
One more time."

Nikos's wet eyes flew to his brave, beautiful wife,
propped on the bed. The strain in her body and the
way she worked with the doctor was something he'd
never forget.

"Ah, there's the head. This guy's got your husband's
black hair."

He heard his wife's shouts of excitement.

"Keep pushing. Here comes Alexandros." Dr. Panos
held the baby up in the air by the ankles and Nikos
heard a gurgle, followed by a lusty cry.

Stephanie started sobbing for joy. "How does he look?" she begged the doctor.

"You can see for yourself after I've cut the cord." A minute later he laid the baby across her stomach and wiped off the fluid. "Come on over here, Papa. You can examine your son together."

As wonderful as that sounded, Nikos leaned over to kiss Stephanie's dry lips first. "Are you all right? I'm so sorry I wasn't there for you."

Her eyes were a blazing blue. "But you have been, all this time, and I've never been so happy in my life. Isn't he beautiful?"

His gaze flew to the baby, who'd stopped crying and gone quiet. His dark eyes looked at Nikos so seriously, reminding him of the way Stephanie sometimes did. He studied the rest of him. His perfect hands with their long fingers were curled into fists. It was like looking through a kaleidoscope, where all the bits and pieces formed a miraculous design. This one was made from the molds of a Walsh and a Vassalos.

Nikos saw Stephanie's mouth and chin, his brother's ears, his mother's black hair, his own fingers and toes, his father's body shape. *My son. My one and only.*

"He looks exactly like you, Nikos."

He turned his head toward her. "You're in there, too. But I want you to know that even if he didn't look like me, it wouldn't matter, because I fell in love with the two of you a long time ago. A miracle happened on the island."

"I know." Tears gushed from her eyes. "I love you, darling. So much I can't begin to tell you."

"No woman ever fought harder to show her love than you did when you came all the way to this remote island to find me. I'll never forget," he said against her mouth. "I've got to tell Yannis. Then I'm going to call the family and tell them they've become grandparents again."

CHAPTER TEN

January 24

YANNIS WAS WAITING for her at the car outside the clinic.
The temperature had to be in the forties. Her sweater
felt good. There'd been some light rain that afternoon,
but now that the sun had dropped into the sea, it had
stopped.

Stephanie had decided to get her six weeks checkup
a few days ahead of schedule, without Nikos knowing.
The whole point was to surprise him.

"Dr. Panos says I'm 100 percent healthy, but I need
to lose weight."

"You look good for a new mother."

"Thank you."

"Now remember our plan."

"Are you sure you want to do this, Yannis?"

He grinned. "Nikos's parents have spent more time
on the *Diomedes* than they have at their house. It's my
turn."

"Alex is crazy about you."

"I love him. Maria and I have been waiting to tend
him. We have it all planned for tonight. Everything's
ready for you on the cruiser."

"Do you think Nikos suspects anything?"

"No. Tassos is with him and so are your parents. Between family, the demands of the business and the duties of a new father, he's too exhausted to be doing much thinking."

She took a shaky breath, so nervous and excited at the same time that she couldn't hold still. "Then I'll just keep walking past the yacht to the cruiser, and wait for him to come."

"When he asks where you are, I'll tell him that after you got back from shopping, you went in search of the camcorder, since you couldn't find it in the lounge. In the end he'll come looking for you."

This was the first night they would be away from the baby. "We'll be in that little cove around the point if there's a problem."

"Don't you worry about anything."

"Alex isn't too crazy about formula, but he'll drink it when he gets hungry."

"Of course he will. It's Nikos you should be worried about. He needs some attention."

She had news for him. *So do I.* "You're an angel, Yannis."

After he'd parked the car at the dock, she gave him a hug, then ran along the pier to the cruiser and hurried on board. There was just one bedroom below. She turned on the heat to warm things up. While she waited, she took a quick shower and changed into a new nightgown her mother-in-law had given her for Christmas.

Though she was already missing her little boy, she was dying to be with her big boy. They hadn't been intimate since her vacation on Providenciales. Right now she was horribly nervous. If he still wasn't prepared to make love to her because of his PTSD, she needed to know before she made herself sick with expectations.

For weeks now they'd shared tender, loving moments with the baby, but Nikos went to bed alone every night like clockwork.

Not tonight!

After leaving the light on in the hallway, she brushed out her hair and climbed under the covers with a novel. For fifteen minutes she kept reading the first page, until she heard him call to her.

"Stephanie? What are you doing? The camcorder was in your bedroom. Come on up. The family's waiting for you."

Her heart thudded too hard. "If you don't mind, I'd like to stay down here for a while."

In the silence she could almost hear him thinking. "Why?"

"Because I'd like to have my husband to myself for a little while."

She heard him come down the stairs. "Are you upset about something?" His voice had suddenly deepened. It did that when he suspected trouble.

"Actually, I am."

He burst into the bedroom. The worried look on his handsome face was priceless. "What are you doing in bed?"

She sat up, feasting her eyes on him. "I've been waiting ten months for you. This afternoon Dr. Panos gave me a clean bill of health, so—"

"You've been to see him already?" he interrupted. If she wasn't mistaken, the news seemed to have shaken him.

"Yes. I couldn't stand to wait until next week. Everything's been arranged. Yannis and Maria are taking care of Alex until tomorrow. I told him we'd motor around the point to the cove and stay for the night. I grabbed your medication earlier today. It's in my purse. So there's nothing you need to go back for. Your parents and Tassos will understand."

A haunted look crept over Nikos's features. "Stephanie—"

"If you have a nightmare, you won't have to worry you're hurting the baby. He's safe and sound on the *Diomedes.* I'm tough, Nikos. I can take whatever happens if you'll give me the chance. I want to be your wife. Won't you let me?"

She watched his throat working. It felt like an eternity before he said, "It's cold on deck. Stay right where you are."

"I promise."

In a few minutes she felt the cruiser reversing. After traveling at wake speed, Nikos opened it up and they were flying across the water. It didn't take long to round the point. He eventually slowed down, and she felt them glide onto the sand in the cove.

More waiting while she heard him take a shower.

Before the light went out, she saw his silhouette in the doorway. He'd hitched a towel around his hips. "I have a confession to make, Stephanie."

Not another one. She couldn't take it. "What is it?"

"When I got back to my unit, I told Kon I'd fallen in love with you, and planned to resign my commission after our mission so I could marry you."

With a moan of joy she climbed out of bed and ran to him, throwing her arms around his neck.

He crushed her to him, scattering kisses over her face and hair. "Forgive me for being so horrible to you. You're the most precious thing in my life."

"There was never anything to forgive. Let's not talk anymore, darling. We've said everything there is to say. I want to make love all night, and the same thing every night for the rest of our lives. You have no understanding of how much I love you."

Nikos gripped her shoulders. His black eyes blazed with desire. "Actually, I'm one man who *does* know. And one day soon, I'm going to do everything in my power to help you find your own father. He deserves to know he has the most wonderful daughter a man could ever be blessed with. I adore you."

"And I, you. Love me, darling. Love me."

They were on fire for each other to a degree they hadn't known in the Caribbean.

As he picked her up and followed her body down on the bed, he spoke the Greek words she'd been yearning to hear him say. Over and over again he whispered, *"Agape mou."* My love, my love.

April 26

"Stephanie? Are you ready?" Nikos walked into the nursery they'd made aboard the *Diomedes*. He was so gorgeous, she almost fainted as he approached in a formal gray suit and white shirt.

"We are!" She looked down at their precious four-month-old Alex, who was so excited to see his daddy he kept smiling and lifting his arms. The two were so handsome it brought tears to her eyes to see them

together. "Guess what, big boy? Today you're going
to get christened."

She expected Nikos to pick him up, but he fooled her
and swept her into his arms first. "I need this before
we go anywhere." Catching her to him, he gave her a
long, passionate kiss reminiscent of their lovemaking
earlier that morning, before the baby was awake. It was
a good thing her eggshell-colored suit with lace trim
was wrinkle proof.

After thinking it over, she and Nikos had decided
the ceremony at the church would take place on the date
of their baby's conception. It was a secret between the
two of them. Knowing Alex was their miracle child,
they'd chosen this particular date to commemorate the
sacred occasion.

They'd asked Tassos and Elianna to be godparents.
Except for the addition of Nikos's mother waiting for
them at the church where they'd been married, it was
like déjà vu to travel there with Yannis and join their
closest friends for the baptism.

Tassos hugged Stephanie before speaking on be-
half of their child, then they followed the priest to the
font, where Nikos's mother took Alex to undress him
and wrap him in a large towel. Stephanie watched in
wonder and fascination as they went through the sacrament of baptism.

After the priest gave him the name Alexandros and
anointed him, Tassos wrapped the baby in a white sheet
and towel. Then Nikos's mother dressed him in his
christening clothes, but as she did so, Nikos's father
suddenly appeared in their circle. He handed the priest
a gold cross and chain to give their baby, the first olive

branch toward a reconciliation with his son. At that same moment Tassos lit a candle.

Stephanie slid a covert glance to her husband, whose black eyes filled with liquid. She grasped his hand before they walked around the font three times. Earlier, Nikos had told her it symbolized the dance of joy.

With the circle complete except for Stephanie's mother, who Stephanie felt was watching from heaven, they witnessed their adorable son's first communion. Stephanie followed Nikos's lead and kissed Tassos's hand before he handed her the baby. Everyone murmured, *"Na sas zizi,"* which meant "life to Alexandros."

They'd planned a party back on the yacht afterward, but for Stephanie the real celebrating was going on right here, seeing the beginning of peace for both families after years of turmoil.

On the drive back to the yacht, Nikos pulled her tight against him. "I have two presents for you, my love. One is a home I've bought for us on Oinoussa. Now that we have a son, he needs a place to play besides the deck of the *Diomedes.*"

She hugged him hard. "I agree."

"Your other gift is in my pocket. I was planning to show it to you tonight, but after seeing my father show up, I've decided I can't wait."

Nikos sounded exceptionally excited. "What is it?" she whispered against his lips.

"The private investigator I hired has found your father."

"Nikos!"

"This is a picture of him." He reached in his breast pocket and pulled out a small photo. The second she saw the dark blond man, she knew it was her father. "We look so much alike!"

Nikos nodded. "He works at a bank in Cheyenne, Wyoming, where he was born. He's married with a son and daughter, who are both in college. When he met your mother, he was on leave from the army. Like me, he had to go back and serve another tour of duty. Four years later he got out of the army and married."

"D-does he know about me?"

"No."

"Thank heaven!"

A look of confusion entered Nikos's eyes before he kissed her. "Why do you say that?"

"Because he's an honorable man who made a good life for himself." Her voice shook. "I don't want to disrupt it. Since Mother chose not to find him, I want to leave things alone." She grasped Nikos's face in her hands. "It's enough to know what he looks like and who he is."

She crushed her husband in her arms. "Thank you, darling, for such a precious gift. What really matters now is our family, our son. I married the most wonderful man alive and I'm going to spend the rest of my life showing you what you mean to me. I love you, Nikos. *I love you.*"

* * * * *

Mills & Boon® Hardback

January 2014

ROMANCE

The Dimitrakos Proposition	Lynne Graham
His Temporary Mistress	Cathy Williams
A Man Without Mercy	Miranda Lee
The Flaw in His Diamond	Susan Stephens
Forged in the Desert Heat	Maisey Yates
The Tycoon's Delicious Distraction	Maggie Cox
A Deal with Benefits	Susanna Carr
The Most Expensive Lie of All	Michelle Conder
The Dance Off	Ally Blake
Confessions of a Bad Bridesmaid	Jennifer Rae
The Greek's Tiny Miracle	Rebecca Winters
The Man Behind the Mask	Barbara Wallace
English Girl in New York	Scarlet Wilson
The Final Falcon Says I Do	Lucy Gordon
Mr (Not Quite) Perfect	Jessica Hart
After the Party	Jackie Braun
Her Hard to Resist Husband	Tina Beckett
Mr Right All Along	Jennifer Taylor

MEDICAL

The Rebel Doc Who Stole Her Heart	Susan Carlisle
From Duty to Daddy	Sue MacKay
Changed by His Son's Smile	Robin Gianna
Her Miracle Twins	Margaret Barker

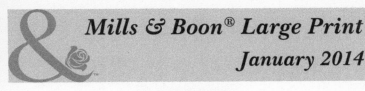

Mills & Boon® Large Print
January 2014

ROMANCE

Challenging Dante	Lynne Graham
Captivated by Her Innocence	Kim Lawrence
Lost to the Desert Warrior	Sarah Morgan
His Unexpected Legacy	Chantelle Shaw
Never Say No to a Caffarelli	Melanie Milburne
His Ring Is Not Enough	Maisey Yates
A Reputation to Uphold	Victoria Parker
Bound by a Baby	Kate Hardy
In the Line of Duty	Ami Weaver
Patchwork Family in the Outback	Soraya Lane
The Rebound Guy	Fiona Harper

HISTORICAL

Mistress at Midnight	Sophia James
The Runaway Countess	Amanda McCabe
In the Commodore's Hands	Mary Nichols
Promised to the Crusader	Anne Herries
Beauty and the Baron	Deborah Hale

MEDICAL

Dr Dark and Far-Too Delicious	Carol Marinelli
Secrets of a Career Girl	Carol Marinelli
The Gift of a Child	Sue MacKay
How to Resist a Heartbreaker	Louisa George
A Date with the Ice Princess	Kate Hardy
The Rebel Who Loved Her	Jennifer Taylor

Mills & Boon® Hardback
February 2014

ROMANCE

A Bargain with the Enemy	Carole Mortimer
A Secret Until Now	Kim Lawrence
Shamed in the Sands	Sharon Kendrick
Seduction Never Lies	Sara Craven
When Falcone's World Stops Turning	Abby Green
Securing the Greek's Legacy	Julia James
An Exquisite Challenge	Jennifer Hayward
A Debt Paid in Passion	Dani Collins
The Last Guy She Should Call	Joss Wood
No Time Like Mardi Gras	Kimberly Lang
Daring to Trust the Boss	Susan Meier
Rescued by the Millionaire	Cara Colter
Heiress on the Run	Sophie Pembroke
The Summer They Never Forgot	Kandy Shepherd
Trouble On Her Doorstep	Nina Harrington
Romance For Cynics	Nicola Marsh
Melting the Ice Queen's Heart	Amy Ruttan
Resisting Her Ex's Touch	Amber McKenzie

MEDICAL

Tempted by Dr Morales	Carol Marinelli
The Accidental Romeo	Carol Marinelli
The Honourable Army Doc	Emily Forbes
A Doctor to Remember	Joanna Neil

Mills & Boon® Large Print
February 2014

ROMANCE

The Greek's Marriage Bargain	Sharon Kendrick
An Enticing Debt to Pay	Annie West
The Playboy of Puerto Banús	Carol Marinelli
Marriage Made of Secrets	Maya Blake
Never Underestimate a Caffarelli	Melanie Milburne
The Divorce Party	Jennifer Hayward
A Hint of Scandal	Tara Pammi
Single Dad's Christmas Miracle	Susan Meier
Snowbound with the Soldier	Jennifer Faye
The Redemption of Rico D'Angelo	Michelle Douglas
Blame It on the Champagne	Nina Harrington

HISTORICAL

A Date with Dishonour	Mary Brendan
The Master of Stonegrave Hall	Helen Dickson
Engagement of Convenience	Georgie Lee
Defiant in the Viking's Bed	Joanna Fulford
The Adventurer's Bride	June Francis

MEDICAL

Miracle on Kaimotu Island	Marion Lennox
Always the Hero	Alison Roberts
The Maverick Doctor and Miss Prim	Scarlet Wilson
About That Night...	Scarlet Wilson
Daring to Date Dr Celebrity	Emily Forbes
Resisting the New Doc In Town	Lucy Clark